Spring Spirit

A NOVEL

Arianna Snow

Golden Horse Ltd.
Cedar Rapids, Iowa

This book is primarily a book of fiction. Names, characters, places and incidents are either products of the author's imagination or actual historic places and events which have been used fictitiously for historical reference as noted.

An *Original Publication of Golden Horse Ltd.*
P.O. Box 1002
Cedar Rapids, IA 52406-1002 U.S.A.
www.ariannaghnovels.com
ISBN 10: 0-9772308-2-1
ISBN 13: 9780977230822

Library of Congress Control Number: 2007923698

First Printing
Printed and bound in the United States of America
by Publishers' Graphics, LLC

Cover: Design by Arianna Snow
        Photography by LCZ, CEZ
        Wallet and lace- Lydia's Remembered
        Layout by CEZ
        Printed by White Oak Printing

Dedicated with love and gratitude to:
God, my family
and
the wonderful librarians
with whom I have had the pleasure
of speaking with over the last years

CE
everything

KAE, CE, LC
editorial

relatives and friends
support

LZ, CZ, SJ and MJ
for bookkeeping and packaging

Agneta Inga-Maj Garpesjo-Davis
Swedish Language Assistant

Mr. and Mrs. Glandorf
for cover contribution

Midwest Book Review
endorsement
♥

HIRAM GEOFFREY MCDONNALLY
FAMILY TREE

PATERNAL GRANDPARENTS
CAPTAIN GEOFFREY EDWARD MCDONNALLY
CATHERINE NORTON MCDONNALLY

FATHER
CAPTAIN GEOFFREY LACHLAN MCDONNALLY

UNCLE
EDWARD CALEB MCDONNALLY

MATERNAL GRANDPARENTS
ALEXANDER THOMAS SELRACH
SARAH GLASGOW SELRACH

MOTHER
AMANDA SELRACH MCDONNALLY

SISTER
HANNAH RUTH MCDONNALLY

NIECE
SOPHIA MCDONNALLY

CARETAKERS
ALBERT ZIGMANN
ELOISE ZIGMANN

SON- GUILLAUME ZIGMANN

FRIENDS
DANIEL O'LEARDON
ABIGAIL O'LEARDON

NAOMI BEATRICE (MACKENZIE) MCDONNALLY FAMILY TREE

PATERNAL GRANDPARENTS
JEREMIAH NORMAN MACKENZIE
OCTAVIA HILL MACKENZIE

FATHER
NATHAN ELIAS MACKENZIE
DAGMAR ARNOLDSON MACKENZIE (STEPMOTHER)

MATERNAL GRANDPARENTS
JAMES HENRY SMITHFIELD
IRENE CLEBOURNE SMITHFIELD

MOTHER
BEATRICE SMITHFIELD MACKENZIE

BROTHER
JEREMIAH JAMES MACKENZIE

DAUGHTER
ALLISON SARAH O'CONNOR

HUSBAND
EDWARD CALEB MCDONNALLY

FRIENDS
HARRIET DUGAN
JOSEPH DUGAN

The Chapters

Chapter 1

"Paper Chase"

"Time will bring you your reward,
Try, try again.
All that other folks can do,
Why, with patience, should not you?
Only keep this rule in view;
Try, try again."

—Anonymous

Edward McDonnally sat, balanced on the ancient stonewall that marked the perimeter of his estate, Brachney Hall. It was the quiet dawning of the first day of March in the year nineteen hundred and fourteen. In a couple of weeks, his bride, Naomi, would join him to share this grand mansion. She had accepted his somewhat unconventional proposal a few months earlier and was now preparing for the move from the small cottage on the outskirts of London with her adopted daughter, Allison.

Edward watched the sun rising silently above the moors, as it offered a burst of flaming color to the grayed meadows stretching before him. Calm with resolution, he reverently observed one of God's most under appreciated miracles. With each degree above the horizon, the morning light revealed the beauty of Scotland's waking spring. Edward was finally at peace with the world, after surviving a series of misadventures with Naomi's engagement ring. He was pleased that the arrangements for the wedding were falling nicely into place, as were those for the wedding reception party.

It has been a long eighteen years...Naomi, dear Naomi. Why did it have to take so long? We have missed so many years together.

The full sun brightened the mist lifting across the meadows. Edward lowered himself down to the ground, slipped his hands into the pockets of his trousers and walked solemnly to the pasture gate. The dew dampened his boots as he plodded toward the white barn, which served as a stable for his two horses. Angus, the gardener and stableman was on temporary leave, visiting with his youngest sister. Edward and

Naomi had discussed hiring a temporary replacement but opted to refrain. The estate gardens and grounds were only beginning to revive from the winter dormancy and Edward, who enjoyed attending to his horses, was on holiday from any business obligations until the beginning of May. The large majestic heads of the Percheron and Hannoverian raised and turned toward the sliding wooden doors with Edward's arrival.

"Good mornin' lads. Slept well? It is another bonny day. I do not know where my young helper is today. Too early for her, perhaps, or maybe it just slipped her mind."

He stroked their faces and ran his fingers through the silken forelocks that fell above the gentle brown eyes of each steed. He blew gently into their nostrils for an equine greeting. Edward carried the flakes of hay from the bin to place in the trough on the south side of the barn to supplement the returning pasture grass. He opened the stall doors through which the two giants wasted no time exiting to enjoy their allotted breakfast. Whistling an old Scottish tune, Edward mucked the two stalls and delivered the load to the pile behind the tool shed. He parked the wheelbarrow and continued down the path to the well to refill the waterer. He began to lower the large wooden pail when he saw a small piece of paper attached to the bucket's handle. After pulling on the rope to retrieve the paper, his large fingers untwisted the wire to release it. He unfolded it curiously. Two words were scrolled cryptically in the lower right corner, "Hammer House." Edward seemed to have a knack for finding himself in unusual situations and this event was running par for the course. This find was unexpected and naturally stumped Edward. He ran his left hand through his sandy-colored hair down over his newly shaven chin. Questioning eyes in the woods watched the confused figure.

"Hammer House...Hammer House?" *Who is the deranged cad that wrote this?* He started to lower the pail into the well's dark cavern when it occurred to him. *The tool chest!* He stuffed the note in his jacket pocket and disappeared into the shed. He knelt down on the dirt floor and slowly lifted the lid to the tool chest, then shut it quickly. *Wait a minute, could this be a trap?* "Ah, no Nathan —I shan't fall prey to your evil doings!" Edward's paranoia with Naomi's vindictive father took hold. He stood up, dusted off his pants and walked briskly through the shed door. He stood outside, momentarily embarrassed, having dis-counted the fact that Nathan still believed him to be dead. Furthermore, he knew that Nathan would never risk returning to Lochmoor. *He would be a fool to show his face,* Edward rationalized knowing that every villager was aware of his connection with Vila Ramsey, the kidnapper of his infant niece, Hannah.

"This is my home and my tool chest!" he acclaimed proudly. The young dark eyes in the forest widened with his bellowing. He vanished into the tool shed with a blurr and flung open the lid. He rummaged through the box, then beneath the wooden drawer, which straddled the top, until another slip of paper found its way into his fingers.

"Ah hah!" He snatched the second piece of paper and brought it to the light of the doorway. The young woman stood hidden within the oaks as she watched Edward examining something too small to discern from that distance.

The note bore, once again, only two words. "Sole cleansing. Sole cleansing?" he reread, noting the spelling of the word "sole". "By George, I have got it!" he announced. He darted across the barnyard, up the brick path to the back entry of the mansion. He squatted down and lifted the bootjack at the threshold. He straightened, placed his hands on his hips, staring and perplexed at finding nothing. "Hmm? Cleansing?" he murmured. The young observer stepped forward into the clearing when she saw the Master of Brachney Hall flip the straw mat and retrieve something from beneath it.

She watched as he held it up to his face. After reading the words, "Sewn Sow" the peculiar man made a mad dash across the yard, back toward the barn. The spectator found Edward's actions to be frantic in nature and disturbingly irrational. Thus, she chose to remain in the shadows of the protective shelter of the trees for the time being. Edward immediately emerged from the building toting a large burlap bag laden with oats. He sat it upright on the mounting block and rolled the top down. Edward peered into the dark depths of the sack and extended his arm beyond his elbow. His fingers began crawling through the grain desperately searching for the next message. This hunt took far greater time and effort. Just when he was about to abandon the pursuit and was considering slitting the bag, the tips of his fingers came in contact with yet another folded paper. The baffled onlooker watched as he pulled it up from the bottom. Lost in the paper trail he gave no more thought to the author of the odd notes and unfolded it and read it hastily, determined to reach the end of this treasure hunt.

There were not just two words this time; he had graduated to four, which read, "Leave no stone unturned". His brows knitted with torment, poring over the multitude of stones stacked innocently in the miles of stonewall surrounding the estate. He shook his head thinking, *No, it cannot end this way.* He reread the scribbled words as the woman waited and watched. *No stone?* He glanced around the estate when the flagstone path leading to the pond caught his eye. He stood silent considering the task ahead, skeptical as to that whether overturning the fourteen stones was actually worthy of his time. The bystander decided that Edward's bizarre behavior had finally come to an end and that she should make her presence known. As she moved the branches away, she was disappointed to see Edward fleeing toward the flagstone path. He flipped the first knowing that it would be too good to be true. Then he overturned the second, which was not harboring the note either. Edward stood up and examined the choices that lay before him.

"I am no fool!" he shouted. The witness to this proclamation had a different opinion. Edward stopped short at the end of the stone path and lifted the last piece, only to find the earthen surface vacant. He stood, threw up his arms in defeat, "That is it! I quit! You have won!" He pulled the aggravating slips from his pocket, tossed them to the ground and marched toward the mansion. Then he stopped dead in his tracks. He took a deep breath and did an about-face. Refusing to be outfoxed by the phantom writer, he shot to the path, randomly flipping the stones with a passion.

The viewer was dumfounded. *Have you gone mad? Are you looking for weevils or slugs! How disgusting!*

The eighth stone proved fruitful, providing the relentless hunter with another clue. He marveled at the words, "Bit by Bit". His heart racing with the thrill of the chase, he darted toward the barn to check through the tack. There, hanging on a nail behind the halters, ironically just above the spot where the grain sack had sat, another note dangled mockingly. He snagged it from the wall and read it with a vengeance. The young girl stood in the clearing anticipating Edward's return, certain that at any given moment he would come zipping from the barn. He did. He ran out to the cart resting by the hitching post, laid down beside it and shimmied under it, between the wheels. The unnoticed visitor's curiosity with the erratic nonsensical display was lost to worry. She scurried towards the cart when her uncle's spurt of wild laughter broke her stride. He continued rolling in the dirt like a raving lunatic beneath the cart; his laughter echoing through the moors.

Sophia McDonnally found the ludicrous behavior to be more than she was prepared to confront. She turned and ran for the woods fleeing to her new home, McDonnally Manor.

She shot through the back entrance of her uncle Hiram's estate, leading from the garden. There she met the housekeeper, Eloise, peeling potatoes in the kitchen.

"Excuse me, Mrs. Zigmann, has Uncle Hiram awakened yet?"

"Yes. He is in the study preparing for a visit to London at the end of the week."

"We are going to London?" Sophia's concern with her great uncle Edward was temporarily removed with news of the trip.

"Miss Sophia, your uncle asked that I might look after," she hesitated. "I meant to say, assist you, while he is in town," the housekeeper reported as delicately as possible.

"I am not a child. I want to go with him. Allison invited me to visit with her and Mrs. McDonnally at their cottage before they moved to Brachney Hall. This is not cricket, I also have business to attend to in town. He never asked if I should want to accompany him," she announced desperately as she plopped down in the chair next to the housekeeper.

Eloise studied the pouting face of the young visitor then returned to her kitchen duty and commented doubtfully, "Not a child?" She smiled down at the vegetables before her. "I have no choice but to do what I am instructed while in your uncle's employ. However, if I were in your position, that of a mature young lady, I would not be brooding out here with the likes of me. I would be presenting my case in the study. Mind you, in a rational, logical manner so as to gain his approval— not as a flighty female."

"You are absolutely right." Sophia pondered and straightened in her chair. "I need strategy." She sat back for a minute deep in thought, then jumped to her feet and gave the unsuspecting advisor a quick hug. "Of course, why would Uncle Hiram want to travel alone, when I am available to accompany him?"

"You will have to take that up with the Master. Off to the study." Eloise gave a brushing motion to send Sophia on her way.

Sophia left with new prospects of escaping the solitude of the moors and venturing back into life in the city, which she was accustomed to in Paris. She hurried down the hall, stopped at the mirror to check her hair, then knocked on the pocket door of the study. A very pleasant masculine voice replied. "Please come in."

Sophia slid the door to the left to find Hiram flipping through a stack of envelopes on the desktop before him. "Good morning, Uncle Hiram."

"Good morning early bird. I did not expect to see you for several hours." Hiram directed his attention back to the envelopes, which he filed through, noting the addresses.

"Uncle Edward said that I could give the horses their morning feeding." She sat in the Duncan Phyfe chair next to him. "Uncle Hiram?"

"Yes, Sophia?"

"About Uncle Edward..."

"Yes?"

"Is he all right...I mean is *he* what most people would consider to be normal?" she asked hesitantly, fearful of offending the loving nephew.

Hiram sat back in response to the unusual question. He cracked a smile and then chuckled. "Edward? Normal?" Hiram stopped to think for a moment. "Edward is quite abnormal. I assure you." Her brows rose immediately. Hiram watched his niece's interest deepen, then lowered his head. "Yes, yes," he folded his hands. "Edward is far from normal...he is the most forgiving, optimistic, charitable person whom you shall ever meet."

"But he was behaving so strangely this morning."

"How so?" he asked nonchalantly.

"He was running between the out buildings, talking to himself. Right before I left, he was laughing wildly, beneath the cart. Uncle Hiram, he was rolling around in the *dirt*."

With this news, Hiram just shrugged with indifference. "My dear Sophia, I must inform you that in regard to your great uncle's actions, there could be a multitude of reasons for his behavior. But I assure you, he is most definitely of sound mind, just a wee bit more animated than the rest of us." He reached over and patted her shoulder gently, "Lay your worries to rest, I suspect that he will regain his composure, after the wedding. After all, he is probably the happiest man alive, now that he is betrothed to Naomi."

"Naomi...Mrs. McDonnally is quite nice. She made me feel very welcome when I arrived. Uncle Hiram, might I ask a rather personal question?"

"No question is too personal for the McDonnally clan. Feel free to ask."

"I am a bit confused, Uncle. I do not understand why Naomi and Uncle Edward are marrying, when...when they did not really care to be married all those years that they were...are. Married, that is."

Hiram straightened, then folded his arms snug across his chest. He peered out the window across the room, delaying his answer to Sophia's unexpected inquiry. The young woman's faced became flushed with embarrassment, sensing that her solicitation was obviously disturbing her uncle.

"Uncle Hiram, I truly beg your pardon. I realize that I am new to the family and that my boldness is inexcusable. I apologize." She spoke with genuine remorse, although tormented with undying curiosity with her uncle's continued silence. "I will leave you now, Uncle," she said, dismissing any hope of joining him on the trip to London and proceeded to the door.

"Sophie, please, sit down, I need to speak with you. You naturally have many questions and you are entitled to proper answers," he invited her, motioning for her to return.

Sophia quite willingly joined her uncle, sitting in the chair to the right of the desk. Hiram took a deep breath and leaned back in his chair to explain the details of his history with Naomi.

"Many years ago, when I was a young lad, a few years younger than you, Naomi and I were...we met. She was uncommonly beautiful then— not that she is not beautiful now. We were close, but I had been forced to leave McDonnally Manor without notice. She then married your uncle, Edward, shortly after the accident, which was responsible for her facial scarring. Edward was an excellent provider for Naomi and Allison, but theirs was not a marriage of love, but rather of friendship. Since then, they have found something more in their relationship. Do you understand?"

"Yes, Uncle. Are you certain that there is no question which you would consider to be too personal?"

"Another one? What is on your mind, love?"

"Would I be wrong in assuming that Naomi's heart once belonged to you?" she asked, overcome with curiosity.

"Your perception is acute, young lady."

"Not really, Uncle, there was something in your eyes. I heard it in your voice."

"The past seems to resurface when you least expect it..." Hiram left his chair and began to pace quietly. He stopped behind the desk chair and grasped the top of it. "Sophia, you are young, and I suspect that you will encounter many loves in your life, for you are beautiful in spirit and appearance. I pray that your heartaches will be few." He pulled away from the chair and began to pace, glancing occasionally at his attentive audience. "It is difficult to conceal feelings of passion and love. Mine were such for Naomi; I loved her with my heart and soul. She was my life. That is why I had to leave her. I was young and had nothing to offer her— no means to give her the life she deserved."

"Were you not the sole heir to the McDonnally estate?"

He paused next to her. "Yes, but there was a misunderstanding of sorts, involving Naomi, Edward, Naomi's father and myself. The details are of no importance, now. My headstrong McDonnally attitude kept me away for almost two decades. If there is one aspect of life that I can advise you, let it be for you to take charge of this inherited cantankerous trait. Do not let it rise up as an obstacle between you and true love."

"And when you returned?" she ventured, just above a whisper.

"Time dictates change. We were different people. The relationship that Naomi and I once shared was obliterated by distrust and bitter disappointment," he added with a hint of contempt.

Sophia's interest increased. She was driven without hesitation to ask, "Uncle Hiram, do you still love Naomi?"

Hiram's head lowered for a moment, then rose with his dark intense stare commanding her fearful eyes to his. A few seconds later, a forgiving smile befell his lips.

"Everyone loves Naomi, Sophie. She is the perfect match for your great uncle. She sets charity above all else. Kindness is her greatest virtue."

Unwilling to overstep her uncle's bounds of privacy, Sophia proceeded cleverly to change the subject and plea her case for accompaniment to London.

"Uncle, I understand that we are traveling to London," she said casually.

"We? I am leaving, but do not worry, Eloise will attend to your needs while I am away."

"But Uncle Hiram, would you not prefer the accompaniment of an entertaining traveling companion? It so happens, that I, too, have business in London."

"How uncanny," he smiled skeptically.

"I have an appointment with Allison," she noted seriously.

"You seem to get along well with Miss O'Connor."

"Yes, once she realized that I was an ally...what I mean to say is that once she realized that I had no designs on Guillaume Zigmann, we got along famously."

"As I do not find it proper to delve into your conjured dealings with Miss O'Connor, I shan't inquire as to their nature. Once again, you have made an accurate reading of my emotions; I abhor traveling alone. I am quite the gregarious type," he grinned.

"Oh Uncle, Guillaume will be— uh, *I* will be forever indebted to you. Now, if you will excuse me, I must pack!" Sophia headed toward the hall.

"One moment, Lassie, save room for the new apparel. Aside from formal wear you will be in need of several riding habits, to join Elizabeth and me on adventures across the moors."

"But I do not know how to ride. I grew up in the city."

"You are a McDonnally, are you not?"

"Yes, Uncle."

"Then you, Miss McDonnally, shall learn to ride."

"Uncle Hiram, you have already provided me with an exquisite wardrobe."

"If I remember accurately, that was winter apparel. Spring and summer will be arriving soon with Miss Elizabeth. She has found Lochmoor quite to her liking."

"That is wonderful, Uncle Hiram. I enjoyed her company. She is a modern woman, very independent. I admire her."

"So do I, Sophia." Sophia hugged her uncle and hurried off to locate Guillaume to discuss her plan.

At Brachney Hall, the laughter ceased. The forty-three year old man lay silent and still in the dust, staring at the underside of the carriage with sheer delight. There above him, was Naomi's message painted in red:

I LOVE YOU, MY MAGIC SQUARE.

Chapter 11

"The Photograph"

"When sleep forsook my open eye,
Who was it sung sweet lullaby
And rocked me
that I should not cry?
My Mother."

—Jane Taylor

Dagmar MacKenzie corresponded regularly with her stepdaughter, Naomi. With the disappearance of her fugitive husband, Nathan, the lonely Swede actively pursued to fill the emptiness of Lochmoor's Grimwald mansion by busying herself with letters to friends and family. In an attempt to brighten the atmosphere with love and laughter, Dagmar invited her three children of her previous marriage, Omar, Olaf, and Gretchen, to visit her home for a few weeks. Their immediate response gladdened her heart and put her disappointment with her husband, temporarily to rest. Gretchen and Olaf, both unmarried, were to arrive within the week, Omar with wife and son, Andrej, shortly thereafter. Dagmar and her children were invited to share in Naomi and Edward's wedding celebration, thus extending the Arnoldson family reunion.

Dagmar set about preparing for the arrival of her adored guests. She hummed a little ditty, which she had sung to her children, while she gave the floors and walls in three of the bedrooms a thorough scrubbing. By midmorning, Dagmar finished her final task with the beds tightly bound with fresh white linen. She stoked the fire and sat down for a much deserved rest in the drawing room. Before her, the fire crackled and the revived flames lifted their heads to peer out between the logs. Dagmar reached down along side of the cozy stuffed chair and lifted her autoharp to her lap. The fingers of her left hand gently depressed the chords into position while those of her right strummed a Swedish lullaby. She sang softly as she played, then stopped with melancholy thoughts that her children were grown, *Mina barn är vuxna..* She paused and spoke, stoically, "So it is," and replaced the instrument by the chair. Within a minute, her newly adopted pup, Flicka, left its quilt by the fire and curled up on Dagmar's lap. The weary woman closed her eyes and fell into a deep sleep. She was dreaming of days past when she was purchasing new shoes for Omar and Olaf in Stockholm.

She awoke at the leaping exit of her pooch and its bark directed at the main door. Dagmar was actually relieved to return to reality, for her dream had developed into a frustrating situation. She envisioned her daughter at her present age, while her sons were small boys. To complicate the nightmare further, Gretchen was adamantly insisting that her very young brothers wore man-sized shoes. Dagmar blotted the few droplets of perspiration from her forehead before pulling her shawl around her shoulders. She left the chair and peeked out the front window to find the approaching postman on horseback.

The mistress of Grimwald exited through the door while drawing the shawl up, snug around her head. She walked down the step stone path, pressing against mother nature's March currents with Flicka at her heels. She waved at the postman, Mr. Kilvert, sitting atop his fine chestnut steed.

"Good morning, Mr. Kilvert."

"Aye, and what a fine mornin' it 'tis, Mrs. MacKenzie. I hae a letter from yer stepdaughter."

He pulled an ivory envelope from his leather saddle bag and handed it down to her.

"Tank you. Naomi is such a sveet girl. She alvays remembers to write. Can ve have tea?" Dagmar smiled with a hopeful smile. "Oh , I have to get de doilies for your vife, anyvay. She vill be attaching de dried flovers to dem for de vedding."

"I would be needin' to stretch me legs and I

would be runnin' a wee bit head o' schedule," Mr. Kilvert obliged and dismounted.

"Oh, dats good!" Flicka took off after a rodent and disappeared from view. "Dun't be avay long Flicka. Mor misses you!"

Mr. Kilvert, like the other residents of Lochmoor, had a soft spot in his heart for the abandoned woman of the isolated Grimwald estate. Since the disappearance of her husband, Nathan, in his attempt to avoid the long arm of the law, the villagers took turns paying calls to the kind mercantile clerk, whenever possible.

Mr. Kilvert smiled as he tied his horse to the small tree at the end of the path and followed Dagmar up the stone steps to the stone mansion.

"Give me your coat," Dagmar insisted as they entered the foyer. She then apologized for her unkempt appearance.

The postman removed the dark woolen jacket. Dagmar placed it on a wall hook on the right side of the door. Mr. Kilvert removed his hat and brushed back the sides of his hair with his fingers while Dagmar removed her shawl and draped it over one of two chairs setting on either side of the fireplace.

"Mrs. Kilvert is vell?"

"Verra well, thank ye. Busy as a mother bird makin' her nest."

"Yah? Getting ready for Yake's vedding?"

"Aye, we are fixin' up the cottage for them. She is there nearly everyday, paintin' and cleanin'."

"Yah, she bought fabric for de drapes last veek."

"Aye, she hung them. It looks better than the main house. I think I will be movin' in wi' them," he chuckled.

"Keeping a big house is a lot of vork. Yake's blessed vit' goot people. Ya vork to keep it clean for de shildren, den day move avay and next ting you know your cleaning for dem to come back."

"Aye, a labor o' love, Mrs. MacKenzie, ye hae been performin' miracles with this one. When Nathan bought it, 'twas a shambles, I heard. Word was that he was goin' to fix it up for his first missus. Ne'r did... Hope ye dunna mind me mentionin' the past?"

"Past it is. I heard dat Beatrice vas a good voman, "Dagmar noted casually and pointed to the left chair. "You can sit here and enyoy de fire vile I fetch de tea." She headed to the kitchen. "I von't keep you long, de kettle is already hot."

Muffled barks at the back entrance diverted her path to let in her closest companion, the scruffy stray pup that chose to live with her at Grimwald, several months earlier. The little dog sensed the presence of the visitor and made a beeline for the parlor.

"Akta dig!" Dagmar's voice echoed from the kitchen, warning the postman of Flicka's return.

A half-second later, Flicka was standing on the visitor's lap licking his face, seemingly propelled by the rapidly fanning tail.

"Hello, I am happy to see ye too," he laughed.

"Come here, Flicka, it is time for your breakfast," the kitchen voice beckoned.

The little canine vanished quickly, leaving the meticulous Mr. Kilvert standing and brushing numerous dog hairs from his "uniform", as he called it. Although his attire was far from professional, he insisted on wearing the same dark gray shirt and trousers for his daily route. His wife had made two more pairs to accommodate the weekly supply; one had suffered at the teeth of a villager's young sheep dog.

Mr. Kilvert scanned the numerous volumes in the bookcase on the right side of the fireplace and withdrew a large illustrated volume of horse breeds. Horses were of particular interest to him and he was delighted to find such a fine compilation readily available. Being a self-taught aficionado of equine history, he resumed his place in the chair with curious delight. He thumbed through the pages of elaborate equine sketches. After studying several drawings, he discovered a photograph wedged between the end of the first chapter and the first page of the second. He adjusted his spectacles and was examining the strange find when the hostess arrived with tea and small Swedish cakes.

"Here ve are. Isn't dis lovely?" She set a copper tray on the small table beside the hearth.

"Vat have you found der, Mr. Kilvert?" She added some peat to the fire. "Help yourself." She reached for the picture in question.

"Hope ye dunna thin I will be intrudin', Mrs. MacKenzie. I was readin' yer book on horses when I found this picture 'tween the pages." He handed her the photo, which she took and sat in the chair across from him.

Dagmar studied the portrait of a young woman with an infant cradled in her arms. She dropped to the overstuffed chair. Dagmar checked the back for further identification. Inscribed on the back were the words:

For Nathan
Surprised to find us hiding in here?
Your loving horsewoman and baby daughter
A chill ran through Dagmar's body.

"Anyone ye know Mrs. MacKenzie?"

"Dis is not Beatrice, of dis I am certain." She sat silent, and then moved to the table to pour the tea.

She revisited the details of her husband's disappearance and possible ties with the old photograph. First, Vila Ramsey, had abducted the infant Hannah McDonnally, Hiram's twin, thirty–five years ago. Dagmar's husband, Nathan, had secretly supported Vila financially, residing in Sweden. Second, there was the hidden grave of Nathan's first daughter, Natalia MacKenzie, found in the Grimwald woods. Nathan paid homage to the memorial, secretly for years. Third, the infant Natalia's mother's identity was unknown. According to the grave marker, Natalia had lived and passed prior to the abduction of the McDonnally baby. Dagmar considered the distinct possibility that Vila may have been Natalia's mother but she had no hard evidence to support it. Dagmar found the date on the photograph to be 1875, the same year that Natalia passed as indicated on the gravestone.

Dagmar raised the linen napkin to her face and dabbed her mouth and asked the nagging question, "Is dis Vila Ramsey, Mr. Kilvert?"

"Vila Ramsey? The woman that stole the McDonnally babe? Ner saw her, we moved here several years after." Dagmar made no response. Noting that Dagmar was disturbed and distracted, the postman prepared to leave. "Thank ye for the refreshments, Mrs. MacKenzie I need to be getting' back to work."

He pulled on his coat and hat and opened the door. Dagmar followed. Once they bid their farewells, Dagmar returned to re-examine the picture. She glared at the solemn expression of the mother in the photograph, piecing together the connecting relationships.

"I must send dis photograph to Naomi and ask her if she knows if dis is Vila, " she mumbled. She ran to the door just in time to catch Mr. Kilvert before he left to continue on his route. "Vait! Mr. Kilvert, I have someting to post."

The postman dismounted and walked back to the mansion while Dagmar entered the study and pulled an envelope and a small piece of writing paper from the desk. She addressed the envelope to Naomi's London address and enclosed a short note inquiring as to the identity of the mother in the photograph. She added a few more lines, then sealed it. She hurried to the door and delivered it to Mr. Kilvert. "I vill pay for de postage later. Dun't lose dis, Mr. Kilvert."

"Dunna worry, Mrs. MacKenzie, tis safe wi' me."

Chapter 111

"The Conspirators"

"A whisper, and then a silence:
Yet I know by their merry eyes
They are plotting and planning together
To take me by surprise."

—Henry Wadsworth Longfellow

Naomi sat on the settee in her soon to be vacated London cottage, admiring the gift from her fiancé, Edward. With the initialed glove pins set with tiny diamonds, her thoughts fell back to the hidden grave of her half sister Natalia, who shared the same initials, "N" and "M". Allison, her adopted twenty-four year old daughter, interrupted the memory, offering two letters that she retrieved from her handbag.

"Sorry, Mummy, I forgot to give you these this afternoon. I was distracted when the postman was discussing his glorious trip to Berlin. He is quite the orator, he hopes to lecture on his travels, someday."

"That lanky young man at the office?" Naomi took the envelopes.

"I would not say that he is lanky. Trim perhaps."

Naomi analyzed the handwriting on the envelopes. She slyly continued her interrogation. "Do you converse often with this gentleman, Allison?"

"Now mother, you know I have been picking up the mail since we returned from McDonnally Manor."

Naomi threw her daughter an approving grin, then quickly clasped the letter opener recognizing the distinct handwriting on the two letters. She did not hesitate to open the envelope bearing Edward's first. Her eyes brightened as she skimmed the first page. "He found the notes, Allison! In order too!"

"That is wonderful Mother. I would hope so, after all the trouble to which you have gone. Does he mention the paint on the horse blanket?" she snickered. "Oh, Allison, you are an old stick in the mud. Let me bask in the success of my treasure hunt."

"You will bask in something else when Edward finds that his prize show blanket is dappled with your success." Naomi ignored the comment and finished reading the letter, then opened the second envelope from her stepmother.

"I wonder how Dagmar is coping." She slid the blade through the end of the envelope. She removed the letter and anxiously unfolded it, revealing the faded photograph. Naomi examined it with Allison peering over her shoulder.

"Who is that, Mother?"

"I have no idea." Naomi quickly turned over the photograph and read the notation to Allison.

"Dagmar says that the date is in the exact time frame in which Natalia lived her short life."

"Mummy, the infant is your sister, Natalia?" she asked in surprise.

"It appears to be, let me see what more Dagmar writes... Kind Mr. Kilvert visited today. While I was preparing the tea, he found this picture in the pages of Nathan's book of horses. Do you know this woman? Is this Vila? Please give my best to Allison."

Neither Naomi, nor her daughter had ever seen a likeness of Vila. Naomi silently read the last few lines, which noted that Dagmar was looking forward to Naomi and Edward's wedding.

"I really need to check into this, Allison."

"Now, Mother, you have a lot of packing and a wedding to tend to. With all due respect, you really do not have time to afford getting sidetracked with another investigation."

"I know, Allison. You have to agree that it is curious."

"Mother..." Allison cautioned.

"I need to show this to Hiram."

"I think that showing it to Edward would be more beneficial, he probably remembers Vila. He was eight years older than Hiram."

"Baby, you are a chip off the old block. Good thinking, I will show it to him as soon as we see him."

"*Chip off the block*, hardly. Mother, when will I find a loyal, trustworthy husband, like Edward?" Allison pouted.

"I think that you have, dear."

"The postman?"

"No."

"Then I do not have an inkling as to whom you are referring, Mother."

"Allison, you know exactly to whom I am referring. The handsome, charming, Mr. Zigmann."

"Guillaume! Agh! I am sorry to offend you mother, but your once dear reading companion is a two-timing pack of lies."

"Allison, you have no evidence on which to base that assumption," Naomi chastised.

"Mother, he is a Casanova. Engaged to two women simultaneously?"

"Allison, he was engaged to only one and that person was not *you*," Naomi regretfully pointed out.

"Exactly!"

"Allison, remember, I was also present the day we left McDonnally Manor when Guillaume stated that he had broken the engagement with Trina."

"Trina...someone should tell her. You know that she is planning a visit to her beloved fiancé."

"That remains to be seen. Enough of this, Allison. Let us go into town for supper."

Hiram and his niece arrived at Naomi's cottage, only to find that the residents had stepped out. Hiram, having experienced more than his share of disappointment, thought nothing of it, while Sophia was thoroughly beside herself.

"What are we to do?" she asked anxiously, pacing in front of the cottage.

"We will call again, tomorrow."

"Tomorrow? I have to speak with Allison tonight!"

Hiram had noticed Sophia's agitation throughout the journey and had expected this very response in the event they did not locate her friend immediately.

"I am certain that whatever the two of you need to discuss can wait for a few more hours."

"No, it cannot. Uncle Hiram, this is urgent!"

Hiram was urging his niece back to the buggy when a figure appeared before them beneath the street lamp.

"Allison!"

"Good evening, Sophia. I am delighted that you accepted my invitation," Allison acknowledged without making any eye contact with Hiram, her companion of a very distant past.

"It was touch and go for a bit, but I resorted to my many feminine charms to persuade him," Sophia announced as she struck a sophisticated pose, then giggled, glancing impishly at her amused uncle.

"I trust your trip was comfortably uneventful, Sophia," Allison inquired maturely.

"Yes, the ride was quite entertaining. Uncle Hiram shared anecdotes from his youth with Great Uncle Edward— but now time is of the essence."

Sophia leaned closer to Allison, "Perhaps we might speak privately?"

Hiram nodded, taking the hint. "I will leave you two ladies to your discussion. I have business to which I need to attend. I will meet you back at the flat, Sophia. Do you have your key?"

"Yes, Uncle Hiram. Tell Elizabeth that I send my regards."

"Do not stay out too late, Sophia."

"Yes, Uncle."

"Miss O'Connor, please see that she returns safely to my flat."

"Yes, sir."

Hiram tipped his hat to the women and returned to the buggy.

Allison led the way into the cottage. After removing their coats, Allison offered Sophia refreshment. While Allison was fetching Sophia's requested glass of water, Naomi returned to the cottage.

"Hello, Sophia, we are glad that you could make the visit," Naomi welcomed her.

"I am honored that you invited me, Mrs. McDonnally."

"Aunt Naomi will be just fine, Sophia," Naomi suggested as she removed her wrap.

"Very well, *Aunt Naomi*," Sophia smiled.

Allison glanced at her mother, "Sophia, we can speak freely in my room. Please excuse us mother." Naomi nodded and continued packing a box of the novels given to her by Mrs. Landseer, her mother's past employer.

"That's quite all right; I have plenty of packing to keep me busy."

The two young women entered the bedroom, which was nearly bare with the exception of two packed trunks, and the bed draped with an heirloom bedspread.

"Please sit down, Sophia."

"Thank you, Allison. You may call me Sophie."

"I prefer 'Sophia', you should too. It is a very elegant name. I should think that I should name one of my future daughters for you. I adore it."

"Thank you, Allison. I am very flattered."

"Now, what did you want to discuss?"

"Allison, I am going to get directly to the point. I naturally was thrilled to accept your invitation to your home, but my visit is twofold."

"Oh? Are you planning to expand your wardrobe, Sophia?" Allison sat down beside her.

"Well yes, Uncle Hiram is so very generous. However, I was referring to another reason. I am here on Guillaume's behalf."

"Sophia," Allison warned, leaving the bed. "I have not the slightest desire to discuss Mr. Zigmann's uncouth behavior with anyone."

"Allison, he truly loves you," Sophia pleaded. He told me so on the day that you left Lochmoor."

"Yes, I know. He made that very clear to me the day— no week— no months that he neglected to mention that he had a fiancé in Paris."

"He does not care for Trina, Allison. He ended that relationship, months ago."

"Then why is Trina planning to go to Lochmoor? A woman does not travel from Paris to visit Lochmoor for cultural advancement!"

"Maybe to return the ring?" Sophia instantly closed her eyes with regret for the comment.

"Not only were they engaged, he honored his promise with a ring? Well, well, is it not odd that I heard nothing of the ring either!"

"Allison, you shan't be so hard on him. Guillaume would do anything for you."

"Anything, except tell me the truth! Sophia, I have had enough experience to know the difference between an honest man and one who is leading a double life."

"Allison, you speak as if Guillaume were a common criminal." Sophia lifted a small pillow from the bed.

"In my opinion, he is— accused, tried and convicted of impersonating a decent human being. Now, this conversation has ended. Have you had dinner yet?"

"No Allison, but I still think that you could talk to him; even criminals get to tell their version."

"Too late. He was given ample opportunities, yet failed to share any of this Trina business with me. As far as I am concerned, Guillaume Zigmann may spend the rest of his life in solitary confinement!"

Sophia let out an aggravated sigh and tossed the pillow down. "Guillaume is not in love with her, Allison. You should pity him, Trina is relentless. She refuses to accept his rejection and is determined to win him back."

"She may have him. We are leaving, now."

"You are not being fair, Allison."

"I beg your pardon? And he was?" Allison left the room.

"Will you not just speak with him and give him a chance to make you understand?" Sophia pleaded as she followed Allison in to join Naomi.

Allison did not answer and Sophia felt the tension building. She chose not to pursue Guillaume's case any further in Naomi's presence. She shrugged slightly seeing the shadow of discontent falling across Allison's face.

"Allison, *there are* people who will not take *no* for an answer," Sophia whispered, making one last attempt to explain Trina's obsession.

"Maybe you are one of them, Sophia."

"I was referring to Trina," Sophia responded, totally annoyed.

"Where would you like to dine, Sophia?"

"The *Crystal Cup* would be nice. We could walk there. It is located on the square, is it not?"

"That will be quite a jaunt," Naomi interjected.

"I have a heavy wrap. I am game if you are, Allison."

"I dined with Mother earlier, but could definitely use some fresh air to clear my head. I will get our coats." The two young women donned their outerwear, bid Naomi farewell and left for the square.

Upon reaching the square, Sophia suggested that they cut across by the fountain. It was not long before the familiar silhouette of a young man came into view.

"What is this? What is he doing here?" Allison demanded emphatically.

"Now, Allison, you see how much he cares for you? Guillaume rode all the way from Lochmoor," Sophia interceded, looking sympathetically to the silent suitor.

"I should not care if he rode all the way from Melbourne, Australia!"

"That would have been a bit difficult," Guillaume spoke up.

"I do not need your sarcasm and I do not need you, Mr. Zigmann!"

"Allison, just let me speak with you a minute," he asked calmly.

"No!"

"What are you afraid of, Allison? The truth?" Guillaume raise his voice a notch.

"The truth? I did not know that word existed in your vocabulary!"

Sophia cut in, refereeing to her best ability. "Now, both of you need to remain calm. Allison, it would not hurt to listen to his explanation."

"Hurt? I am tired of being hurt! Interesting scheme that the two of you conspirators devised. How clever you two are. I expected more from you, Sophia!"

"I will show you!" Guillaume retaliated.

"No, Guillaume! Stop!" Sophia pleaded as he flipped open his jacket and jerked out a small box, only to look up in time to witness his beloved Allison storming down the street with no regard to alarmed passersby while she plowed through the crowded walkways. Guillaume, was about to toss the ring into the fountain, when Sophia commanded once again.

"No, Guillaume!"

Guillaume reconsidered and pulled a coin from his pocket. He stepped up on the fountain wall and leaned forward.

"She is the most obstinate woman that I ever met. I thought Trina was incorrigible. I could use a change of luck."

With the toss of the coin, he lost his footing and fell into the fountain, which sent Sophia into hysterical laughter. Guillaume pulled himself up and despite the shock of the chilling experience, he joined in the merriment.

"Do not make me laugh when I am so utterly

depressed," he snickered.

Sophia quickly offered a hand to the dripping friend. Guillaume studied the outreached hand remembering Naomi's memory of young Allison. Allison had offered the same generous gesture to a bullied boy in this very fountain and to him when he fell at McDonnally Manor some months before.

"I seem to be down more often than not." He climbed out, drenched from head to toe.

Sophia smiled, not quite sure what he meant by the comment, except possibly in reference to his defeatist attitude.

"Sorry this evening was such a disaster, Guillaume."

"Oh Sophie, do not blame yourself. My procrastination has delivered my fate once again. Had I been straight forward with Trina, she would be out of my life and had I been honest with Allison, she would still be in it. I never wanted to hurt either one of them," Guillaume looked forlornly at his waterlogged boots.

"I think that is very admirable."

"Thank you, but look where it has left me. Here with you."

"Well thank you, Mr. Zigmann, your candor is greatly appreciated," Sophia scowled.

"No, that is not what I meant. I appreciate your efforts."

"I know. We should get you up to Uncle Hiram's flat to dry out."

"No, not your uncle's. I will go down to the station."

"Guillaume Zigmann, are you so proud that you would prefer to catch your death, rather than face my uncle?"

"Sophie, you cannot possibly understand. I

should die first *before* I would make a fool of myself in his presence again."

"Again, Guillaume?"

"Never mind, I will be fine. I could use some hot tea. Which café do you choose?"

"You are being irrational."

"I am all right, I know you mean well," he amended as he wrung out his trousers and caught a sneeze on his sleeve.

"Well, let us get you inside. Come on, my proud friend," she took his right arm and led him down the street towards the Crystal Cup Café.

Once they arrived and observed the well-dressed clientele, Guillaume admitted, "Sophie, I shan't go in there, look at me."

She studied his dishevelment and nodded in agreement. "You are right. We had better find someplace a little less formal."

Meanwhile, Allison passed two cafes before entering Mrs. Greville's *Berry and Leaves,* now quaintly lit with candles on the tables beneath the windows. Still steaming from the altercation with Guillaume, she pushed in the door with excessive force and marched over to the counter. The proprietor lost her pleasant smile to a concerned expression. Allison hastily scanned the chalkboard.

"Hello Miss O'Connor...I have missed you," Mrs. Greville greeted cautiously.

"Good evening, Mrs. Greville. May I please have a cup of the house tea? It is nice to see you too," she added somewhat embarrassed by her cool entry. "I am a bit at odds with the world today."

"My dear, there are no troubles too large for my tea to tame. Any sweets for you?"

"No thank you," she replied handing the gentle woman a few coins."

"Thank you, take a seat Miss O'Connor, I will bring it to you."

Allison, after closing her purse, walked instinctively to the table at the far end to take a chair, when she noticed the table was already occupied. Her brows rose with surprise and confusion.

She began to leave when the patron's convincing hand enclosed around her wrist.

"Wait, Allison, please sit down."

Allison closed her eyes, breathing deeply; she refused to make any further contact with her captor.

"Please, Allison."

She relented, took two steps back, and sat down across from the familiar dining companion.

Not far away, Guillaume and Sophia approached the very same quaint teashop. Guillaume reached for the door handle when he spotted the familiar couple looking seriously at one another.

"She talks about me! Look at her— in record time she is back in his arms! I have a notion to go in there and give her a piece of my mind!"

Sophia looked puzzled, with her friend's accusations in seeing Allison sitting across from her uncle Hiram.

"Back in *his* arms? Guillaume, they are just conversing."

"I doubt it. She is probably gloating."

"Guillaume! What are you thinking? Allison hardly knows my uncle."

"Sophie, you are so young and naïve. She just could not be happy with someone her own age. No, she had to have the *Master* of McDonnally Manor."

Guillaume peered in the window again. "This has opened my eyes. This spat was not at all about Trina, it was about her unleashed desires to be with that middle-aged—"

"How dare you Guillaume Zig—"

"What did you say?" an approaching woman's voice abruptly cut off the niece's defensive anger.

Guillaume and Sophia turned to face the disheartened expression of Elizabeth Clayton, the woman who Hiram had become very fond of and had made the decision to move to Lochmoor to open her business.

Guillaume shook his head and reiterated, "You might as well know the truth, Miss Clayton. Allison and….Mr. McDonnally, they were…before he met you. Do you see the jacket that she is wearing?"

Elizabeth nodded.

"He bought it for her," Guillaume said with disgust.

Elizabeth raised her brows, with curiosity.

Sophia cut in, "Now see here! Guillaume you are terribly mistaken— it was Naomi that he…" she swiveled around and looked with concern toward Elizabeth who cocked her head and now wore a displeased frown.

Guillaume responded quickly to the remark, "Yes, yes, Sophie, it was the mother, the daughter, it is every woman! He is not at all discriminating!"

Sophia retorted, "That is slanderous, Guillaume!"

"Perhaps, but it is true," Guillaume stood firm.

"Excuse me, I need to be going," Elizabeth said just above a whisper. Then turned and rushed down the street.

In the café, Hiram remembered flashes of his short-lived relationship with Allison: the first day that he met her at this very cafe, *she was wearing red then, too.* Then there was the day at Kensington Gardens beneath the statue of Peter Pan where she gave her first monologue, *she was a delightful Wendy* and all those evenings they practiced the foxtrot, *she was so sweet and tolerant of my mistakes.* Then the memories darkened when they leapt to that dreaded day on which he discovered that she was Naomi's daughter; the day in the garden where he broke her heart.

"Hello, Ja—, Mr. McDonnally." *Will I ever forget you as Jack?* She thought with further irritation.

"Good evening...or is it?"

"It is none of your concern," Allison snapped.

"On the contrary, where is my niece? I left her in your charge."

"Sophia is fine. She is as fine as any woman can be in the presence of Mr. Zigmann. She needs to tend to her *own* affairs and leave me to mine."

"Mr. Zigmann?"

"Yes, do you know that he had the nerve to follow me to London and to present me with an engagement ring when he is already engaged to that French woman!"

"I should say that I am not surprised," he said calmly.

"What? And you find that acceptable?" Allison retorted. "Deception is unacceptable!"

"Allison, have you not forgiven me?"

Allison stared into the teacup steaming before her.

Arianna Snow

"Allison, please, do not let our past be the source of Guillaume's punishment," Hiram suggested with sincere concern.

Allison stood up, sneered at Hiram, snatched her bag and marched for the door. Hiram sat motionless, then wiped his forehead with the linen napkin, tossed it down and left the table. He half-smiled at the astonished Mrs. Greville and then left to meet with Elizabeth.

Chapter IV

"Number Eight"

"And wilt thou leave me thus,
And have no more pity
Of him that loveth thee?
Alas! Thy cruelty!
And wilt thou leave me thus?
Say nay, say nay."

—Sir Thomas Wyatt

Hiram closed the door of the narrow brick building and removed his cap. The uninviting odor of dust and ancient rotting wallpaper hung in the hall of countless treads and risers that stood before him. The worn wooden staircase suffered from the apparent weight of many weary residents, who had struggled to return to their flats after a hard day's work. The dreary atmosphere failed to dishearten Hiram. Armed with a box of the finest chocolates and anticipation of seeing the lovely Elizabeth appear from behind the closed door on the upper flat, he mounted the stairs. This was his first visit to Elizabeth's home since she moved from her room above the Gillian's art gallery. Hiram had never suspected her embarrassment for the shabby condition of her humble abode, when she engineered the modification of meeting places in the past. Now, it was the last thing on his mind.

Reaching the top step, he paused to collect his thoughts, straighten his hat and to smooth his beard. He took a cautious breath that irritated his nasal passages. This initiated two abrupt coughs expelling the dusty air. He cleared his throat, gave his head a slight shake, threw back his shoulders and proceeded to the door of flat number eight. The tarnished brass numeral was barely visible in the dim lighting. He closed his eyes for a moment, envisioning, Elizabeth, the forlorn young artist sitting at the art exhibit and her signature on the painting depicting an elderly woman knitting. His genuine smile awaited her response to his sharp rap on the door. The door cracked slightly open.

"Hello, Hiram."

"Good evening, Elizabeth," he returned cheer-fully.

"Hiram... I have reconsidered. I really think that it would be for the best if I were to stay in London."

"Until spring?" Hiram asked, somewhat confused.

"Permanently."

"Permanently? I thought that you enjoyed your stay in Lochmoor."

"I did, it is a beautiful village, but I think that I would be more content, here in London."

"Elizabeth, have I done something to offend you?" Hiram asked with confusion to her attitude.

"Hiram, I really am very tired. I would rather not discuss this any further."

"May I see you tomorrow, Elizabeth?"

"I think not, Hiram. It would be best if we went our separate ways. We come from different worlds."

"But Elizabeth— "

She closed the door. The sound of the locking latch cracked in Hiram's ears like a gunshot. His muscles tensed yet he stood helpless, incapable of defending himself from this tormenting fate. The volcanic outrage was slowly building in his attempt to understand Elizabeth's rash decision. He was glued to his position in front of the door. The thick dismal hall air crept around the motionless figure until the unpleasant atmosphere stirred him back to the reality of the situation. He did not belong there; this was his past revisited as a lost recluse, not a proud member of the McDonnally clan. He placed the box of chocolates at the threshold of the door and stood up to face the numeral eight. The rejection bore down with overwhelming intensity, making him taut with anger and shock. His right fist slowly rose to knock but stopped in midair. His arm dropped to his side.

Hiram stepped back from the door, pulled his gloves from his pocket and pulled them on, fighting the feelings of embittered disappointment that defied his retreat. He stood tall, chin up, and then tipped his hat to the numeral eight.

"Goodbye, Miss Clayton," he gnashed his teeth and made an abrupt exit for the stairs. Midway to the next landing, he turned and looked to Elizabeth's door. Appalled, he saw a small rat scampering over the box of chocolates. A momentary reflex to retrieve the candy was lost to his disgust with the entire situation.

Hiram moved swiftly through the streets. His boots fell to the rhythm of the disturbing words, pounding in his head— *different worlds, different worlds, different worlds.*

He made straight way for Daniel's flat to confer with his dearest friend. Skipping every other step of the back staircase, Hiram's long stride delivered him to Daniel's flat above the bookstore in seconds. He rapped gently, then harder, as no one responded. A moment later, the door cracked open.

"Who is it?" Daniel inquired.

"Hiram. Daniel, sorry to disturb you but I need to speak with you.

"C'mon in ole boy, what's troublin' ya?" the robed figure offered.

"Daniel, I cannot understand women," he confessed, removing his hat and tossing it on a chair. "Everything was going like clockwork. I thought that I knew her and she ended the relationship without warning," his voice rose.

"Elizabeth?"

"Yes."

A young woman clad in a long, white cotton

nightdress appeared from the bedroom, yawning and stretching.

"Daniel, what is all the ruckus?" she asked.

Hiram turned to the unexpected voice with surprise and immediately snatched his hat.

"Daniel, I apologize, I —"

"No, no, Hiram, 'tis only my sister, Abigail. She may not sound Irish but she is— from the top o' that fiery head down to her wee toes."

"Miss O'Leardon," Hiram bowed slightly.

Daniel's sister looked over the visitor.

"Abigail, 'tis a private conversation, please go back to ya bed." Abigail scowled and disappeared into the room.

"Daniel, I apologize, I had no idea that you were entertaining guests."

"Not guests—"

The voice from the bedroom interrupted calling out, "I am just his one and only sister!"

"Go back to sleep, Abby!" Daniel insisted. "Now, Hiram, what has happened, explain to me slowly, man."

"Maybe I should let you get back to sleep, Daniel."

"No, no I was preparin' the cot when ya called."

Hiram sat down in a chair next to the cot.

"Very well. Elizabeth— we were getting along famously and then tonight, when I arrived at her door, she acted as though I had the plague. She refused to invite me in and—"

"Probably entertaining a guest of her own!" Abigail called out.

Hiram left his seat with the unexpected remark.

"Abigail!" Daniel returned, vexed with his

sister's behavior.

Hiram's attention darted angrily toward the bedroom doorway.

"I highly doubt that, Elizabeth *is* a refined woman!" Hiram defended.

"O' course she is," Daniel agreed. "Go on, Hiram."

Hiram made a double take of the bedroom entrance and continued, "She gave no explanation, with exception to some gibberish about our worlds not meshing. She nearly closed the door in my face. Daniel, I do not know what to think? Something has happened to change her. I am sure of it," he began to pace.

"She is not worthy of you!" the feminine voice echoed. Hiram stopped.

"Abigail, stay out o' this, I shan't warn ya again!" Daniel demanded. The brother's face was now flushed with fury.

The woman flew from the bedroom before the bewildered guest.

"What are you, a man or a sniveling—" Abigail complained. Daniel cut her off.

"Abigail, I insist that ya return to yer quarters." His sister ignored his demand and stood firm in front of the towering figure.

"Howard, no woman wants a whining, insecure—'" Abigail began.

"The name is 'Hiram'," Hiram protested.

"No matter, how wonderful can she be if she never gave you the opportunity to explain, Henley?"

"Hiram! Miss O'Leardon, I really do not think that this is any of your concern."

"I am a woman and—"

"I never doubted it, miss."

"I have the advantage of knowing how a woman thinks, unlike my brother," she turned and glared at Daniel who now sat with his head in his hands defeated and embarrassed.

"That woman does not care two shillings for you," she shook her finger up at him.

"You have never met the woman and cannot possibly judge her or her behavior," ridiculed Hiram.

"Facts are facts and you need to face them!" she shouted. "A handsome man of your means does not need the likes of that fickle female. How ridiculous!"

"Ridiculous? Who is calling whom ridiculous? You are professing to be an expert on human behavior and yet you are standing in front of a perfect stranger in your nightclothes, giving instruction on how to handle women," Hiram countered.

"*Perfect* stranger? Hardly, Hyatt..."

"Hiram!"

"Abigail!" Daniel reprimanded.

"Go ahead. Make a fool of yourself. Crawl back to her and beg for mercy and forgiveness and take her a peace offering of *chocolates,* perhaps," she snickered. The "chocolate" comment set him off.

"How dare you!" Hiram bellowed.

"Hiram, Hiram," Daniel intervened, "she' is young and doesna know what she is sayin'," as he ushered his struggling sibling from the room.

"I am not young; I will be twenty and seven in June!"

"Twenty and seven and not married and *you* are advising me?" Hiram called back.

"Twenty and six!" her voice echoed from the back of the flat.

After an exchange of very few words, the bedroom door slammed and Daniel returned.

"Sorry, ole man, I dunna know what possesses her sometimes."

Hiram shook his head, "I will not comment on that statement. I should leave. I have to meet with my niece."

"Hiram, maybe there is some truth in what my sister says," Daniel suggested casually.

"What!"

"Maybe Elizabeth is not the woman for ya. Abigail speaks her mind. She means no harm. She *can* be quite the proper lady."

Hiram raised his brows in question, and then put on his hat. Daniel let him out.

"Me friend, think it o'er. We will talk tomorrow, o'er breakfast. Sleep on it."

Hiram nodded, "Good night, Daniel."

"Good night, Hiram."

After the door closed, Hiram walked slowly down the stairs. The window above him opened and Abigail appeared. She whispered down to him.

"Hiram?"

"Yes?" he frowned.

"Mark my words, she is not worthy of you," she smiled coyly and closed the window.

Hiram shook his head and pulled on his gloves. He continued to his flat to meet Sophia. He unlocked the door and spotted his niece's coat hanging in the hall.

"Sophie!" he called and removed his gloves.

"Uncle Hiram, I am in here by the fire."

Hiram removed his hat and overcoat and hung them next to hers.

"Hello, Sophia. And how are you this evening?" Hiram inquired, filling a goblet with the water decanter on the small desk by the window.

"Actually, my visit was a disaster of the worst kind. Poor judgment on my part, maybe I should not have come to London with you."

Hiram turned to his forlorn niece, curled up in a chair under a soft, brown coverlet. After drinking half the water, he commented sym- pathetically.

"I am sorry you were disappointed, I know that you were looking forward to the meeting."

"Uncle Hiram, you would not have believed it. I had the best intentions and the evening went from bad to worse, as it progressed. First it was belligerent Allison, then Guillaume quarreling with Allison, then Guillaume and the fountain."

He sat down in the chair across from hers. "Yes, I would believe it," he replied listening to the description matching his own experience.

"When I arrived, I thought that I could convince Allison to at least speak with Guillaume. She refused to speak with him. Can you imagine that?"

"I can do more than imagine it."

"There he was, so handsome and sweet, with a surprise for her and she just stopped him cold, acting like they had never meant a thing to one another. Do you understand how he felt?"

"Completely, like they never cared for each other."

"Frankly, I was appalled and embarrassed to be associated with Allison. She was so very unfair to him. He deserved the right to be heard at the very least," she straightened in the chair. "Do you not agree, Uncle?"

"Most definitely, Sophie— very unfair."

"I tried to get him to come up here to dry out, but he refused. He's very intimidated by you, Uncle."

"Who is?"

"Uncle, Hiram! Guillaume, of course." Sophia reiterated, perturbed with her uncle's distraction.

"Oh, yes, Guillaume," Hiram tried to reconnect the bits of information that his niece had provided.

"I will tell you, I was glad that he did not agree to stay with us after his negative comments to Elizabeth at the teashop."

Hiram straightened abruptly in his chair.

"I knew that what he was saying could not possibly be true, but I have never known him to lie; they were only nonsensical comments. He was so inflamed when he saw you with Allison that he just lashed out. Guillaume is like that, acts first, and thinks later. He found a room at the inn to dry off and I suggested that he—" Sophia's sentence was cut off with her Uncle's renewed interest.

"Sophia, exactly what did he say to Elizabeth?" He left his chair and loomed over her.

"Oh, I am not quite sure of his *exact* phrasing, but something to the effect that there was some undesirable triangle between, you and Allison and her mother. Can you believe that? But, you shan't fret over their break up, Uncle, I am really beginning to question Allison's suitability for Guillaume, at this point, anyway."

"Triangle! The nerve of that lad!"

"I would not worry about it; Elizabeth just seemed to ignore it all and went on her way."

"Ignore it? You can thank your friend, Mr. Zigmann, for destroying any chance I had for a relationship with Elizabeth!" Hiram began to pace.

"Uncle?"

Hiram stopped and faced his niece. "Miss Clayton made it crystal clear that she does not care to see me anymore."

"What! Did she give an explanation?"

"Some petty comments. I *knew* there was something more," he hit his fist into the palm of his other hand and continued pacing across the room.

"What are you going to do, Uncle Hiram? Do you want me to speak with her, woman to woman? I can explain that you and Naomi are just friends and that Guillaume had no right to insinuate that you ever had a personal interest in her daughter," Sophia offered with sincerity.

Hiram paused and looked in wonder at his niece for her innocent offer. After a deep sigh, he sat down in the chair across from her. "I think we need to have a talk."

"Another one?" she inquired with concern.

"I have to admit, what Mr. Zigmann implied is not altogether untrue."

The young woman's eyes widened, "No, Uncle...not Allison too?" Sophia exclaimed as she shed the coverlet and stood defiantly before him with definite disapproval.

With her unexpected snap response, Hiram quickly added, "I was not aware that she was Naomi's daughter."

"But Uncle, Allison is only a couple years older than I am," Sophia cringed with disbelief.

"Sophia, our relationship was platonic, we were just good friends," Hiram said sharply.

"But Uncle, why were you secretly meeting with her at the café tonight?" Sophia's voice elevated slightly.

"Hold on, young lady. What are you implying by *secret meeting*?" Hiram demanded. Sophia snatched the coverlet.

"This is none of my concern!" She threw a piercing stare to her guardian. "Good night, Uncle Hiram." She exited the room mumbling, "Poor Elizabeth," and closed the door to the bedroom.

"Poor Elizabeth? What about me! She's the one that would not let me explain!" He dropped to the chair. "*No one* will give me the opportunity to explain! *Women*," he muttered.

Chapter V

"Abigail"

"I saw her
upon nearer view
A Spirit,
yet a Woman too!"

—William Wordsworth

The next morning Hiram entered the parlor at his flat and eyed a sheet of stationery propped against the brass candlestick on the mantle. He opened it and read the following note from his niece.

> *Uncle Hiram,*
> *I have gone to the square to meet with Guillaume before he returns to Lochmoor. Feel free to dine with anyone of your choosing. I will be joining Guillaume for breakfast.*
> *Sophia*

Hiram folded the note, rolled his eyes and tossed it into the fireplace. He went to the hall, lifted his overcoat and hat from the hall tree, and slipped them on, feeling irritated and unjustly judged. He checked his pockets for his gloves and locked the door behind him. When he reached the bottom step Mrs. Yonnovich, the landlady, greeted him cheerfully.

"Good morning, Mr. McDonnally. It is a brisk one today. I would hope that you have your gloves. Should you not be wearing them?" She then vanished into the vacant flat below his.

"I have them in my—" he began to explain, disturbed that she was now out of earshot. *Will anyone give me a chance to explain?* He jerked his gloves from his pocket, pulled them on and tightened them down between each finger, scowling with frustration.

When he reached *Daniel's Den,* he noticed the new Zane Grey novels displayed in the window. *Perhaps, I should relocate to America,* he thought bitterly.

The tiny brass bell jingled when he entered Daniel's store. Daniel rose from behind the heavy walnut table stacked with the latest editions of Dickens' classics.

"Top o' the mornin', Hiram."

"Hello Daniel, I would like to purchase a Zane Grey novel for my uncle. He is quite the fan of American western fiction."

"It would be me pleasure." Daniel plucked a copy from the stack in the window, wrapped it in brown paper, and handed it to Hiram.

"What do I owe you?"

"Not a penny. After last night, I would be owin' ya."

"That is not necessary, Daniel."

"Yes, 'tis. I will get me hat and coat and notify Oliver." Within a couple minutes, Daniel's young assistant was seated at the counter, unwrapping the new shipment and Hiram and Daniel were bracing the March wind. Upon reaching the entrance of their favorite café, the memories from the prior night urged Hiram on to the next, *The Crystal Cup*.

"What goes on here, ole man?" Daniel inquired following his dear friend.

"I need a change of atmosphere, Daniel."

"'tis not a good idea, Hiram," Daniel warned.

"Mrs. Greville shan't mind. We frequent her café several times a week."

At the café, the two men waited to be seated while Daniel glanced nervously around the room. A young woman dressed in a crisp black uniform with a spotless white apron greeted them and led them to a table set for four. Once seated, Hiram reviewed the menu while Daniel continued to scan the area. The waitress returned to take their order. Hiram placed his first. Daniel decided hastily and sat preoccupied.

"Daniel, I would like to take this opportunity to apologize for last night. In an attempt to make amends I would like to extend an invitation to you for a holiday at my home in Lochmoor."

Daniel's jaw dropped as he peered above Hiram's right shoulder.

"Why Mr. McDonnally, how generous of you," a sweet feminine voice announced on Hiram's right. Hiram turned to meet the prim and proper countenance of Daniel's sister, Abigail. The lovely and sophisticated appearance before him softened Hiram's shock and surprise. Her beautiful fiery red hair was neatly pinned with ringlets framing her face. Her form-fitting red and black plaid suit flattered her fine figure. Daniel and Hiram immediately stood with her arrival.

"But have you forgotten? My brother is entertaining a guest." Abigail looked disapprovingly to her brother. She continued, "Oh, I beg your pardon, not a *guest,* merely a blood relative." The two men exchanged glances and then Hiram offered the peeved woman a chair.

"Miss O'Leardon, would you care to dine with us?" Hiram asked reluctantly, maintaining his dignity.

"If you wish. It seems that my brother neglected to notify me that he would be dining here this morning." She turned to Daniel who was looking to the breakfast crowd for escape.

"I am certain that it was only a slight lapse in memory," Hiram suggested and stared suspiciously at the silent brother who responded with a slight shrug. Hiram lifted his hand to signal the waitress and then graciously requested a menu for the new guest. Abigail placed her order expeditiously and then sat silent. Hiram decided to ease the tension after several long minutes.

"I trust you slept well, Miss O'Leardon?"

"As well as one can expect, considering the disruption. And you, sir?"

"I cannot say that my hours of sleep were *restful.*"

"I am sorry to hear it, and why not, pray tell?"

"If you must know, Miss O'Leardon, I was preoccupied with a number of issues."

"Ah, still brooding over Elizabeth," she stated confidently.

"I beg your pardon?" Hiram went on the offensive.

"Abby!" Daniel objected.

"Mr. McDonnally, do you need the town crier to announce that the relationship is dead before you will abandon it?" Abigail unfolded her napkin.

Hiram abruptly stood up and threw his napkin on the table. "Excuse me, I need to speak with the proprietor," he announced sternly.

"Wait a minute! I may not be a McDonnally, but I have as much right to eat here as anyone!" Abigail proclaimed, scrunching the napkin.

Hiram leaned toward her. "Please lower your voice, Miss O'Leardon, or you *will* be asked to leave. I was about to inquire as to the delay in our service." Hiram's serious expression broke into a playful grin, having succeeded in putting the woman in her place for the first time.

Abigail humbly replied, "Of course," and refolded her napkin.

Daniel, now flushed with embarrassment took the opportunity to speak privately with his sister.

"Abby, Hiram is me best friend in all the world. I will not be toleratin' this behavior any longer. Do ya understand?"

Abigail, annoyed with her brother's loyalty to Hiram, folded her arms in a huff, brooding quietly.

A moment later, Elizabeth Clayton entered the café. Upon seeing Daniel, easily spotted by his orange tufts of hair, she proceeded to the table, knowing that avoiding Hiram's best friend would be more awkward than greeting him.

"Hello, Daniel," she said nervously.

Daniel stood, "Good mornin', Miss Clayton. This is me sister, Abigail."

"My pleasure, Abigail. Elizabeth Clayton." Elizabeth smiled sweetly.

Daniel looked to his sister, expecting the worst.

"Elizabeth! Well, what have you to say for yourself?" Abigail demanded.

"Excuse me, but I have no idea as to what you are referring," Elizabeth answered sharply.

"I believe a woman should speak straight forwardly, no beating around the bush, nor playing fickle games with unsuspecting gentleman!"

Annoyed by the stranger's accusations, Elizabeth nodded to the blushing brother, "Daniel, if you will please excuse me, I should be going to my table now." Elizabeth turned to leave, only to run smack into Hiram. The shock of the contact with his dark, unforgiving glare sent her fleeing from the restaurant. Daniel resumed his place, ready to explode. Hiram peered down objectionably to his defender and returned to his seat next to her. Noticing that the other customers were amused by the confrontation, Hiram explained to Abigail in a hushed tone.

"*Please* leave me to attend to my own affairs, Miss O'Leardon. I can fight my own battles, thank you."

"You apparently need all the help that you can enlist, Mr. McDonnally." Abigail responded, determined to get in the last word.

Daniel bit down on his index finger to refrain from using a series of unacceptable comments.

Hiram knitted his brows in contempt and cleared his throat to retaliate when the server arrived with their order. The three ate without speaking for several minutes before Abigail casually questioned her brother.

"What is your decision, Daniel? Are you accepting the invitation to the famed McDonnally Manor or are you staying in London with your only living blood relative?"

"Only livin' relative? What 'bout our cousin Rupert?"

"Rupert? He does not count."

Hiram searched Daniel's face for explanation, but Daniel just rolled his eyes up.

"Well, are you leaving London, my dear brother?"

Before Daniel had a chance to reply, knowing he was doomed either way, Hiram defended his position.

"You obviously misunderstood my intentions, Miss O'Leardon. I was not attempting to disrupt your visit with your brother. Daniel is free to schedule a visit to Lochmoor anytime that he finds convenient."

"Did you hear that Daniel? The Master of McDonnally Manor has graciously granted you the honor of determining your own schedule."

"Of course, Daniel may do as he wishes," Hiram's voice raised a notch.

"I am certain that Daniel will choose to accept your invitation without regard to the likes of me. I do plan to stay in London indefinitely. But I can manage quite well, alone at the flat above the bookstore while my brother is enjoying the amenities of your estate."

"*Abby...*" Daniel pleaded.

"Miss O'Leardon, I was not purposefully singling you out. If you choose to join your brother, so be it," Hiram relented and took a bite of a scone.

"Certainly not! I am not in the habit of soliciting invitations for personal convenience." Abigail's golden brown eyes pierced Hiram's.

Hiram wiped is mouth with his napkin, "Most assuredly not," Hiram agreed and the three returned to their meals.

Daniel prayed that the meal would be finished without further disturbance when Hiram inquired.

"Miss O'Leardon, would a personal invitation to my estate meet your approval?"

Abigail sat down her fork and looked up in surprise. Daniel was now convinced that his friend was a glutton for punishment.

"Perhaps...sir."

"Miss O'Leardon, may I have the honor of your presence for a holiday at my home? You may bring Daniel along, if you so desire," Hiram grinned.

Abigail looked to her brother, hiding her smile beneath her napkin. Daniel nodded skeptically.

She placed her napkin across her lap. "If you so desire, Mr. McDonnally," Abigail accepted nonchalantly and returned to finish her meal.

Hiram continued with his meal harboring mixed feelings with Abigail's acceptance. The challenge was invigorating yet the potential for disaster laid in wait in each conversation with this woman.

By ten o'clock, the threesome finished their breakfast. Hiram offered his arm to Abigail and the trio left the restaurant. Once outside the door they met Sophia and Guillaume.

"Sophia," Hiram greeted.

"Uncle?" Sophia looked inquisitively at his breakfast date, glowing on his right.

"May I present—"

His niece interrupted. "I beg your pardon, but we are in an awful hurry. We have only a few minutes before Mr. Zigmann is scheduled to leave." As they brushed by, Hiram nodded at Guillaume who returned with, "Mr. McDonnally," and an attentive smile toward Abigail.

After the encounter, Hiram apologized to Daniel and his sister for his niece's rude behavior and accompanied them back to the bookstore to finalize the plans for their visit.

Hiram returned to his flat displaying his gloves and a warm smile for Mrs. Yonnovich who was dusting the balusters on the landing. He spent the final hours of the morning seated before the fire contemplating the series of misadventures of the past twenty-four hours. After dipping the pen in the inkwell at the table, he lowered it to a piece of note-paper and began to write.

My dear Elizabeth,

He sat silently mulling over every possible explanation when he slid a line through Elizabeth's name. He held the pen motionless for a minute, then dipped it again and began writing on another page.

Abigail

Hiram and Sophia ended their stay in London a few days early. Their relationship improved with the shopping spree for Sophia's new wardrobe, for any conversation of Hiram's personal affairs had remained latent for the time being. Once they returned to the flat, Sophia opened each of the many packages that her uncle had juggled up the stairs. She examined each new outfit, anticipating the days ahead that she would don them. In a short while, the parlor was strewn end-to-end with the finest women's apparel in London. After proudly savoring the bounty, the grateful niece ran to embrace her uncle for his unmatched generosity.

"Bless you, Uncle Hiram!" My mother and I thank you from the bottom of our hearts."

"You are quite welcome, Miss McDonnally, the pleasure was most definitely all mine. But now, we must repack your treasures and prepare to leave."

"Yes, Uncle." Sophia began folding a suede riding jacket and breeches. "Uncle, who was that woman, the red-haired one?"

"If you would have stayed a minute longer, I could have properly introduced you. I *was* disappointed in your attitude, miss."

"Sorry, Uncle."

"She is Daniel's younger sister, Abigail. She is somewhat unpredictable, but good-hearted. She is a true spring spirit. I have invited them to visit Lochmoor."

"*Spring spirit,* Uncle?"

"Yes. Abigail can be as abrasive as the March winds, yet I feel that she has a special hidden beauty, not unlike that which nature reveals each spring."

"What about Elizabeth, have you given up on her entirely?"

"Sophie, I told you, it was Elizabeth's choice to separate, not mine."

Sophia continued to fold the outfits and replace them in their boxes. "Uncle Hiram, will we ever see her again? I enjoyed talking with her on our last visit. I like her."

"So do I, but I really doubt that our paths will ever cross again," he said somberly as he stacked the boxes by the door.

Edward stood beaming in the drive at Brachney Hall as the cart carrying his little family came into view. His grin broadened to its dimpled limit when the cart pulled up along side of him, delivering the two delighted women. Naomi reached for his extended hand, and then withdrew it.

"You shaved off your beard!"

"Do you mind?" He offered his hand. Naomi placed hers in his and stepped down.

"Not at all. Goodbye, Lucas McClurry, *hello* Edward Caleb McDonnally."

Edward pulled Naomi close to his chest and kissed her without reservation. Naomi fell into his welcoming gaze, "Hello, love. I have missed you."

"Me too, you silly woman. I hope you are proud of yourself, with your paper chase."

"Admit it, Edward McDonnally. You loved it."

"Well, most of it, except—"

"Mother, I told you that he would notice the blanket," Allison could not help but interrupt.

"The blanket? Did I miss something?" Edward asked. Naomi took the opportunity of his distraction to flee for the safety of the mansion.

"Naomi!" he called after her while Allison watched the mystery unfold with an impish grin.

Once inside the foyer of Brachney Hall, Naomi caught her breath until her fiancé arrived a second later. Naomi was unbuttoning her coat when Edward assisted in lifting it from her shoulders, "Naomi, to what blanket was Allison referring?"

"Now, Edward, never mind that, I have something that I need to show you." Naomi pulled Allison aside and whispered. "Allison, when we show him the photograph, we cannot make any comment alluding to the identity of the woman as Vila. We shan't influence him in any way."

"Yes, Mother," Allison humored Naomi. Naomi casually lifted the photograph from her handbag, holding it for Edward's inspection.

"Edward, dear, do you know this woman?"

"Well, well, what do you know?" Edward grinned as he stared at the picture.

"You recognize her?"

"Of course, I know her. I am surprised that the black sheep allowed anyone to photograph her."

"So, it is really *her?* "Look closely. Edward, are you positively certain?" Naomi demanded.

"Quite. I have not seen her since I was a child, but I *am* certain. I would know those braids anywhere. I am surprised to see her photographed with a child."

"Did you hear that, Allison? It is she. It is Vila! This is unbelievable. Do you know what this means, Allison? We have to inform Dagmar."

"Mummy, I take back everything that I ever said about your questionable ability to solve mysteries. You are a genius! Well, with Dagmar's help."

Edward listened to the energetic dialogue between mother and daughter with increasing bemusement.

"Vila Ramsey, I always wondered what she looked like. Edward, the baby is my half-sister, Natalia. It is obvious by the date on the back," Naomi explained.

Edward flipped the photograph over and read the inscription. "Naomi, what made you think that this was Vila?"

"Actually, I have to give credit to Dagmar. It was her hunch, knowing of Nathan's history with Vila and his keeping Natalia's short life a secret. Edward, do you think that it is possible that Nathan helped Vila kidnap Hannah because she was distraught over the loss of her baby, Natalia?"

"Maybe, Naomi, maybe."

While Naomi and Allison settled into their temporary home at McDonnally Manor, Daniel and Abigail took the opportunity to do some sightseeing before they made their journey to Lochmoor. Before leaving London, Daniel took Abigail to Buckingham Palace, the Tower of London and completed the tour at St. Paul's Cathedral. As they rode along the Thames River, Daniel reminded his sister, "When we get to Lochmoor, ye have to mind yer manners. Ye are givin' Hiram a poor impression of the O'Leardon women."

"Poor impression? Daniel, I do believe that you are becoming crotchety in your old age. I simply believe that a woman has a right to speak her mind."

"Hiram is a proud man and does not enjoy bein' led around like a paradin' pony, Abby."

"Nor do I, brother."

"Remember, we will be guests in his home."

"I only have one fundamental problem with Mr. McDonnally: he is your typical male. You are concerned about my impression? If your dear friend thinks for one minute that I am like every other woman who is impressed with his wealth, social position, charm and good looks, he is in for a rude wakening."

Daniel shook his head and threatened, "If ye dun't be behavin', there will be more than one Abbey left in Westminster."

As they traveled north, they visited Birmingham, then the Nottingham castle. They continued to Manchester to visit their cousin Rupert. The hillsides were dotted with black-faced sheep, and beautiful stone cottages. Abigail loved the Midlands and vowed to live there someday.

Chapter VI

"Crow's Nest"

"And the Raven, never flitting,
still is sitting, still is sitting
On the pallid bust of Pallas just
above my chamber door
And his eyes have all the seeming
of a demon's that is dreaming,
And the lamp-light o'er him streaming
throws his shadow on the floor;"

—Edgar Allan Poe

The loss of Naomi's "first" engagement ring, which Edward purchased for her a few months earlier, lingered in his memory. So much so, that each outing, which led him across the MacBride Bridge, demanded that he stop long enough to make a quick visual search for the missing jewel which fell from Joseph Dugan's hand, that fateful night. Although the ring had little sentimental value, replaced with the multi-gemmed band that Naomi wore proudly, its exorbitant monetary value ate away at his natural frugality. Although he was quite charitable with his fortune, he avoided foolish investments and made purchases only after adequate evaluation. The loss of the valuable ring seemed senseless to Edward. Its sale could have contributed to a great deal of good for those less fortunate than himself. He vowed that if he ever were to find it that, he would donate the proceeds to a worthy cause. If not, he prayed that whoever found it would be deserving of its value.

With each recurring search, Edward's imagination went wild considering the possible candidates for finding the lost treasure. His mind raced from the vision of a small child's delight, holding the sparkling gem to that of the greedy expression of the village miser, Mr. Chisholm. The strange little man spent most of his afternoons in search of "misplaced" items that he could resell for a handsome profit. Occasionally Edward's charitable side would picture a tearful vagabond on his knees by the stream's edge scooping up the elaborate ring.

The next day, after another fruitless pursuit by the water's edge, Edward mounted his Percheron to return to Brachney Hall. "Onward, lad," he instructed. He continued across the rolling hills admiring the seasonal changes in the countryside, recapping the afternoon consultation with Harriet Dugan about his wedding gift for Naomi. Naomi had mentioned, in passing, on several occasions, that she was intrigued with the artistry, time and effort that was involved in producing patchwork quilts. With this in mind, Edward commissioned Harriet's sister, Helen, to design one of the intricate coverlets to present to his wife. Many quilting circles in Britain highly recommended Helen's work and recognized it as professional. Unfortunately, Helen remained in her birthplace, the village Innesgreen, deep in the Highlands. Her choice of residence made personal contact with the quilter, infeasible and impractical. Harriet had agreed to make detailed notes on the desired design and had sent them to her sister on Edward's behalf. Now, upon completion, the finished product would be sent to the village mercantile with the other specialty items that Dagmar had ordered for the local villagers, not as adept in their handiwork as Harriet's sister.

On the porch of the caretakers' cottage for McDonnally Manor, Guillaume sat at his parents' home oblivious to the chill surrounding him.

Allison, why do I waste my time on you. He reached into his vest pocket and pulled out the ring box. The torn covering clung to the rusted tin casing. The dip in the fountain in the square and his negligence had virtually destroyed the case. He lifted the lid revealing the delicate ring inside. It, on the other hand, had not suffered in the slightest, but in the eyes of the observer, its luster was lost. He snapped the lid closed and shoved it into his coat pocket and headed for Brachney Hall to discuss the matter with his comrade and mentor, Edward. After a brisk walk, he arrived a few minutes later to find Edward standing on a ladder leaning against the trellis on the south side of the mansion.

"Edward, what are you doing up there?" Guillaume asked anxiously, instinctively moving in to brace the ladder.

"Hello, Guillaume. I am trying to get a better view of that crow's nest in the oak tree."

"Why, are there eggs in it?"

"No," Edward stared and stretched to the left holding one hand on the ladder and the other on the trellis.

"Edward, at what are you looking?"

"One moment, I think that I see something." Edward leaned a few more degrees to the left, barely holding the rungs with his fingertips. "Guillaume, go to the barn and fetch the riding crop. It should be long enough."

"The crop, Mr. McDonnally?"

"Yes, Guillaume, please go, quickly."

Guillaume reluctantly let loose of the ladder and ran to the tack room to retrieve the small whip. He found it propped up against a bag of grain and rushed back to assist Edward.

Edward moved cautiously down the rungs and thanked Guillaume as he made his way back up the ladder with the crop. When he reached the fourth rung from the top, he leaned out with the small whip extended in his left hand. To his dismay, he had miscalculated and the crop was a couple feet too short.

"Blast it! Too short! Guillaume fetch the lunge whip."

"Yes sir." Guillaume shot back to the barn in

search of the lunge whip. In seconds, he was heading back with the long whip in hand. Edward exchanged whips half way down the ladder. Guillaume grasped the side of the ladder as Edward climbed to reposition himself. Edward, armed with what he considered to be the right tool for the right job, stretched as far as he felt safe to the left, with the whip as an extension of his left arm. Guillaume watched the long black whip wavering as it moved toward the nest and as Edward inched slowly toward the left of the rung. However, the dried mud from Edward's soles flaked off, falling into Guillaume's eyes, as he tried to steady the ladder. Guillaume blinked violently to discharge the aggravating particles. Edward leaned and reached to the left as Guillaume let loose with his right hand to wipe the dirt from his eyes. Edward's weight pulled heavily to the left as the ladder's right side left the ground and veered toward the tree. Guillaume fought to support the sixteen-foot ladder but failed as Edward let out a yell.

Edward fell with the ladder to the ground below followed by the nest caught by the whip. Edward's flailing body crushed Guillaume beneath it. Both men lay silent. A glistening black wave swooped down to the fallen men. Through Edward's clouded vision, he discerned the form of the dark demon before him peering at the ring a few feet from his face. Staring at the immobile figure, the crow cawed with seemingly sheer delight in mocking the victim of its folly and scolding for the destruction of its home. In the blink of an eye, it plucked up Naomi's first engagement ring in its beak and flew up into the oak.

"Son, how do you feel?"

Guillaume looked hazily to his mother's face and fell back to sleep.

"Nothing to serious, Mr. and Mrs. Zigmann; a cracked rib and mild concussion 'tis all that he suffers. He will be needin' to take it easy for a while. The taped rib should heal without difficulty. No heavy lifting, Albert," Dr. Kelly advised Guillaume's father. Albert agreed.

"How is Edward?" Eloise, Guillaume's mother, asked.

"With a broken leg and arm, he is a wee worse for wear," Dr. Kelly informed her.

Naomi returned from the kitchen with a pitcher of cool water.

"I want to thank all of ya for helpin' with that makeshift gurney, to be gettin' these two inside," the doctor said. "It could hae been much worse." He shook his head.

"We all thank *you,* doctor. We are just grateful that you were visiting Lochmoor." Naomi returned.

"Ay, we can be thankin' Maryanne and her babe. The Wheatons are gettin' 'head o' me, I have only five," the doctor chuckled.

Naomi joined Edward, lifted his head, and helped him sip the water. "Oh, Edward," she placed her cheek next to his, "you could have been killed," she sniffled. Edward was silent for a minute then he placed his *good* right arm closed around her. Tears formed in his eyes.

"I am so sorry, Naomi, for my foolishness. I have spoiled our wedding plans," he whispered.

The doctor and the Zigmanns looked sympathetically to the couple sharing a tender moment on the other side of the room. The road traveled to their wedding day had been a difficult one up to now and with the matrimonial date set only a week away, postponement was inevitable.

Another remorseful face appeared in the hall from the kitchen. Its possessor carried a basin of warm water and a stack of white cloths. She walked silently to the younger patient and knelt beside him. She dipped a soft cloth in the basin, rang it out and placed it across Guillaume's forehead. She sat absorbed in his quiet face. She bit her bottom lip trying to hold back her tears. Her hands trembled as she removed the cloth and turned it over and replaced it. Eloise watched as the young nursemaid cared for her son.

You do love him...He really is a good boy. He never meant to hurt you, Eloise thought. She looked down at Guillaume resting quietly on the cot. *My poor boy, thank God you are all right.*

The doctor spoke with Albert in the kitchen and recommended that Guillaume remain at Brachney Hall for a few days until his concussion symptoms subsided. Dr. Kelly knew that Eloise's separation from her son would be difficult, but reassured her husband that Guillaume was not seriously injured. Dr. Kelly ran a series of tests on Guillaume's physical and mental faculties to determine his condition. The patient had awakened long enough to give coherent answers to the doctor's questions, including, knowing his name and successfully giving a detailed description of the accident.

"Dr. Lambert will be returnin' in a few days to check on them," Dr. Kelly assured." I will be leavin' him the reports of their conditions."

Down the road at McDonnally Manor, Hiram and Sophia arrived, relieved to be home again. They found a note, with a brief summary of the accident, tacked to the front door.

"What does it say Uncle Hiram?"

"Edward and Guillaume were in an accident, they are at Brachney Hall with the Zigmanns. Quickly, get back into the carriage." Hiram and Sophia, both concerned with the condition of the two victims, climbed into the carriage and headed straight away for Edward's home. Their arrival sent the two dachshunds barking at the main entrance where Dr. Kelly greeted the couple on the front steps.

"Good afternoon, Mr. McDonnally, Miss McDonnally."

"Good afternoon, Dr. Kelly," Hiram and Sophia replied in unison.

"How are they?" Hiram asked anxiously.

"Your uncle suffered the greatest injuries. His left side is out o' commission wi' a broken arm and leg and a number o' bruises, but no injuries to his head or organs."

"Thank God," Hiram sighed. "And young Zigmann?"

Sophia held her breath.

"His were of a different nature. When the ladder fell, it caught the edge o' his chest wi' Edward's weight on it. It cracked a rib. It is a miracle that his lungs werena crushed. He did take a severe blow to the head and has a slight concussion, noted by his blurred vision. However, he is coherent and his speech is fine."

On hearing both reports, Sophia burst into tears and ran through the mansion door. She was taken aback to find Allison teary-eyed at

Guillaume's bedside. She then ran to her great uncle's side.

"Oh, Aunt Naomi," Sophia whimpered.

"We are glad that you are home, Sophia," Naomi greeted her.

"Oh great Uncle Edward," Sophia sobbed.

"Now, now, you are correct, Sophie. I am *great*. You need not worry," Edward grinned.

Sophia squeezed his right hand and placed a kiss on his cheek. She wiped her tears with a hankie from her handbag and then hurried over to the Zigmanns, gathered by Guillaume's cot. She exchanged understanding glances with Allison and ran her finger down Guillaume's face.

"You belong together, Allison." These were Sophia's only words. Then she sat quietly holding Guillaume's hand.

"I will be off to see Mrs. Wheaton, now. Take care all," Dr. Kelly waved. Albert escorted him to the carriage and watered the McDonnally horses waiting in the drive.

The accident was not an approved topic for conversation by order of the Master of Brachney Hall. After Edward refused to explain his motives for being on the ladder, Hiram remained seated next to his uncle and made harmless jokes about Edward's track record with the *unusual*. He reassured Edward that he would hire extra help to maintain Brachney Hall and offered his assistance with the upcoming nuptials. Naomi found the discussion of the wedding to be trivial at this time; her dream of the celebration at Brachney Hall had faded with her sole concern being that of Edward's recovery.

Edward extended his gratitude and then inquired, "How is Elizabeth? Will she be arriving soon?"

The mention of Miss Clayton's name spurred a fleeting glance from Sophia and a moment of hesitation for Hiram. "She is well, Edward," was the only information Hiram deemed necessary to report. "Eloise, I have invited a friend of mine to the manor. Of course, I had no idea that you would be preoccupied with your son, at the time."

Eloise's attention was drawn to the end of the room. She sipped her tea without concern.

"How nice, Hiram. Elizabeth is coming for a visit?" Naomi asked, happy to see Hiram severing himself from his past life as a recluse.

"No, not at this time. I have invited Daniel O'Leardon, my dear friend— the Irishman who owns the bookstore in London."

With this news, Eloise nearly choked on her tea. She swallowed hard and looked to Naomi with shock. Eloise's reaction momentarily confused Naomi, having known Daniel for years. Then it hit her. She put two and two together and came up with the Daniel of Eloise's 'freckleswept' infatuation of the past. Eloise had confided in her that the second meeting with Daniel, decades after the first, had been difficult for Eloise.

Naomi's perplexed look turned to one of equal surprise and concern. *Poor Eloise, how will she ever manage being in such close quarters with Daniel?* Naomi thought observing her helpless friend.

Hiram witnessed the shock waves passing between Naomi and his housekeeper. "I apologize for the short notice. Is this going to be a problem Mrs. Zigmann?"

Eloise sat speechless, searching the tea leaves in the bottom of her cup for an answer. Then one word left her lips, "Guest?"

"No, I further apologize. *Guests,* two to be exact."

"He is bringing...a wife, Hiram?" Naomi ventured to guess.

Eloise closed her eyes and prayed. *Dear God, please, not Daniel and his wife. Please do not put me through the freckleswept test.*

"No, Naomi, Daniel's younger sister. Daniel never married."

This could be worse. He is not married, Eloise panicked. Naomi went to the housekeeper's side.

"Not to worry, Eloise, I will see you through this," Naomi promised.

"Ladies, I had no idea that inviting a couple of guests would become such a monumental event. I realize the timing is poor," Hiram added.

"No Master McDonnally, I am not complaining. The rooms and meals shall be in order," Eloise said dutifully.

"I can hire additional help if need be, Eloise," Hiram offered.

"No, sir, I can manage," Eloise feebly added.

"Very well then. They will be arriving the day after tomorrow," Hiram announced, satisfied.

Eloise fainted dead away.

*"They know not I knew thee,
who knew they too well:—
Long, long shall I rue thee,
Too deeply to tell."*

—Lord Byron

Chapter VII

"The Attack"

"So all my thoughts are
pieces but of you,
Which put together makes
a glass so true
As I therein no other's face
but yours can view."

—Michael Drayton

The next morning, just after dawn, Eloise, carrying the lantern and metal cans, met Eck Grahame with the horse drawn milk van. After a brief exchange, Mr. Grahame filled the cans and pulled his leather pouch from his coat. He withdrew his book and recorded the dairy delivery to the McDonnally account. Eloise bid him "good morning" and held her early vigil to check on Guillaume at Brachney Hall. She was delighted to find her son in the dining room, sharing tea and scones with the very attentive, Miss O'Connor. The young couple was making small talk and light of the accident, despite Edward's objections. At this point, no one was aware of Edward's motives on that dreadful day.

Allison looked to Guillaume with pity and concern as she had that first day at McDonnally Manor. He was once again the innocent stumble-bum with good intentions, but whatever his failings, she was eternally grateful that his life had been spared and his injuries not severe. After a short conversation with the young pair, Mrs. Zigmann left her son, comforted that Guillaume and Allison's reunion seemed relatively secure.

Eloise had mechanically dusted and prepared the guest rooms with fresh linen. She had sprinkled the carpets with damp tealeaves to absorb the dust. The meals were planned and several sweets, covered with parchment paper waited in the pantry to welcome Daniel and his sister, Abigail. Eloise's remaining household duties were temporarily on hold until the next morning when the specter from her past would reappear.

Although the sun rose that morning like any other, for Eloise Zigmann, it marked the onset of further mental anguish and distress as the

upcoming meeting with the man of her past drew
nearer. She poured a cup of tea, wrapped her shawl
around her shoulders and went directly to the
cottage porch. She sat down in the wicker chair and
began rocking without any thought to the normally
soothing movement. She focused on two isolated
trees standing peacefully in the pasture vacant of
any animal life larger than a rabbit or gray squirrel.
Her thoughts were directed elsewhere.

*Daniel O'Leardon, coming here to McDonnally
Manor,* she thought feeling helpless and doomed.
She never believed that her last meeting with
Daniel in the train station, some twenty years ago,
would be their final encounter. She struggled with
the embedded guilt that Daniel's speckled face had
'freckleswept' her into abandoning her sister that
day at the train station.

She considered the oddity of some relationships, which hang on like cobwebs in the memory,
and of the fact that a small world it truly is. *How
strange that he is the Master's dearest friend.*

She knew that under no circumstances could
she afford to lose her composure. Officiating as the
"greeter" was solely her responsibility. For the first
time in her employ, she was dubious about
successfully carrying out this seemingly simple
duty. She lamented the inability to predict Daniel's
first response of their meeting. She knew with this
information, she could at least arm herself with the
proper defense. However, the truth of the matter
was that she was undeniably at Daniel O'Leardon's
mercy.

*If only I was fortunate to share a moment
alone with him before we met with the others. I could
explain to him that it would be beneficial to both of
us to keep our relationship a secret.* She dropped her

head with further despair, guilt-ridden, knowing that secrets were her husband's pet peeve.

How will I manage, without revealing our past? She glanced up towards the estate garden when the falling watering can hit the bottom step with the aid of the curious pooch, Heidi. Naomi appeared, gathered up the mischievous pup and waved to Eloise.

She knows, Eloise thought, not quite comfortable sharing her dilemma with even her dear friend. *Thank goodness. I did not tell Harriet or all of Lochmoor would know about Daniel before he ever arrived.*

Eloise waved and sipped her tea, now cooled from the spring air. Eloise had considered several choices in handling the awkward situation, none of which was pleasant. Like the Master, her husband, Albert, did not have a clue as to her past with Daniel. Confessing to her husband could intensify the already uncomfortable meeting.

Maybe Daniel will not let on that we know each other. She frowned feeling that concealing the relationship would be misconstrued as deceitful, alluding to the possibility that there was more to it than there really was. All the same, her regrets for the incident at the train station, as innocent as it was, were great. "Glory be, there was not anything to it!" she remarked in her defense.

"Wasn't anything to what, Ellie?" a boisterous voice startled her. She turned to her husband, now standing on the edge of the porch, peering out at the two horses cantering across the field from the barn.

"Oh, nothing. How was your catnap, Albert?"

"Fine. I am ready to take on the world."

"I left Guillaume a half-hour ago. He is resting quietly. I am pleased that Allison has patched up things with him. She has done wonders with lifting his spirits. He was moping around here, for what seemed like eternity, brooding over their break up."

"Miss O'Connor is a fine young woman. She has a touch of fire, like you Ellie. Men like a woman that keeps life interesting."

"I hope so, Albert," Eloise mumbled in regard to *her* situation.

"What did you say dear?"

"I am glad that you approve of Allison. She may become a member of the family in the not too distant future."

"Yes, only if our son has learned his lesson that secrets are destructive. I fear that poor woman will not tolerate too much more from him."

Eloise cringed with his remark.

"And one more accident and she will believe that he is a walking calamity."

Eloise agreed, "Yes, it seems that he has certainly had more than his share of misfortune. First, the attack, then his fall, and now this."

"He shall consider himself blessed that she still has a place for him in her heart."

Eloise quickly changed the subject, "I saw the carriage. It is quite beautiful, Albert. You did a superb job polishing it."

Thank you my dear, and might I return the compliment? McDonnally Manor looks fit for the queen. Maybe I should say *king.*"

Eloise got up from the rocker to take the teacup to the kitchen when Albert asked, "What do you know of this friend of the Master's?"

Eloise stopped breathing and dropped the cup to the porch floor. The crashing cup and Eloise's blank stare drew an immediate response from her husband.

"Ellie are you hurt?"

"No doubt as to where our son gets his clumsiness." Eloise fingers trembled recovering the broken pieces.

"Careful not to cut yourself, now," Albert lovingly warned, picking up the last couple of pieces. Eloise began to cry with the pressure of the predicament resting heavily upon her. "Oh, my dear Ellie, it is just a cup, I will buy you another one," he looked sympathetically down to her.

"No, Albert, I have had them for years. It is not necessary," she argued, driven by the guilt of her dilemma.

"Fine, I always say, out with the old, in with the new. After the guests leave, we will go down to the mercantile and have Mrs. MacKenzie show us her finest dishes. You may pick out any set your little heart desires," Albert comforted.

"I do not deserve them, Albert," she wept.

"Yes, you do. It was only an accident."

"It was no accident!" she cried out and ran to the kitchen. She carried shards of the cup, not unlike those elements of her past, prone to cut deep. He sighed and followed her. Albert was not quite certain of the best method to handle his wife's erratic behavior, contrary to his son's confidence in his father's omniscience in dealing with the opposite sex.

Albert made no further inquiry concerning the guests and carried out the morning chores, oblivious to the impact the new arrivals would have on his wife's state of being.

That afternoon, Albert drove Sophia to the village to pick up the mystery package that Edward had ordered several weeks earlier for Naomi. Sophia entered the mercantile and reached down to pet Dagmar's excited little dog, Flicka.

"Hello, Flicka. Good girl. Mrs. MacKenzie, may I take Flicka out to visit with Rusty? He is out in the cart with Mr. Zigmann. I am caring for him while Guillaume is convalescing."

"Yah, send her out. How is de young man doing?"

Sophia opened the door for Flicka and answered, "Oh, he has to be careful for awhile until his rib mends."

"Yah, ladders and men dun't mix?" Dagmar dropped her head and wiped her hands on her apron, "I lost my broder from a fall."

"How dreadful, I am so sorry," Sophia said with concern.

"Yah, he was painting a sign for de voolen mill. A vind caught him like a sail and sent him flying. Dose men should be very grateful to have survived."

"They are, Mrs. MacKenzie" she closed the shop door as Flicka joined Rusty, now running playfully under the cart. "Mrs. MacKenzie, I am here to pick up a package for my great uncle Edward."

"Yah, it is here, in de back room. Von minute, please."

Sophia picked up the brightly painted wooden candlesticks from the counter, admiring the fine Swedish designs.

Dagmar returned with the package, "Der from Sveden, here's de package."

"These are beautiful." Sophia smiled and placed the candlesticks back on the counter. "I am considering them as a wedding gift for Uncle Edward and Naomi."

"Der de only vons. I vill set dem back for you."

"Thank you, Mrs. MacKenzie."

Dagmar handed the large box tied with twine and placed the candlesticks on the shelf beneath the counter. "Please send Flicka back in."

"I will. Good day, Mrs. MacKenzie and thank you." Sophia's curiosity with the contents of the box was nearly unbearable, but she dare not open it.

"Give, everyvon my regards," Dagmar called out to Sophia as she left the shop.

"I will." Sophia led Flicka back into the shop and gave a short wave to Dagmar who was assisting Mrs. Kilvert with fabric for a tablecloth for Jake and Agnes' cottage.

"Wait here with Rusty, Sophia. I will be right back." Albert climbed down from the cart and entered the mercantile. A few minutes later, he returned carrying a large carton.

"What is that, Mr. Zigmann?"

"A surprise, Sophia."

"Oh…" *Another one! I do not believe that I can bear much more.* Sophia's imagination went wild, on the trip back to Brachney Hall, considering the possibilities of the unknown treasures hidden within the packages.

When they arrived at the estate, Sophia jumped from the cart and Albert handed her the box. En route to the portal, Angus, the gardener, came around from the south side of the mansion to meet her.

"Miss McDonnally, the Master instructed me to hide the package in the maid's room. It willna be a surprise if Mrs. McDonnally sees it."

"How delightful, a surprise for the bride-to-be!" Sophia handed the package to Angus.

"Albert!" the gardener called out.

"Angus," Albert nodded.

Sophia returned to the cart. "Please, tell Uncle Edward that I shall call on him later. I have business to attend to now."

"Verra well, Miss." Angus waved and walked stealthily along the side of the mansion. Sophia giggled as she saw the elderly man creeping on tiptoe toward the backdoor.

Just as they were to leave, a glistening object below the large oak caught Sophia's eye.

"Wait!" Sophia insisted.

She jumped down from the cart and ran to the brilliant object. She picked up the most beautiful ring that she had ever seen. She held it up to the light when a crow sitting on a branch in the oak above her cawed frantically. Sophia ignored its warning and headed back to the cart with the treasure. The crow dived down from the tree, skimming past Sophia's head. She screamed and clamored into the cart.

Albert swung the whip at the menacing bird, "Get out of here!" The frustrated creature retreated to the treetop. "Are you all right, miss?"

"Yes," Sophia said weakly.

"Hang on! I need to get the cart back home before three, to drive Eloise to Grimwald. We have about two minutes." Sophia placed the ring in her pocketbook and held on while Albert snapped the reins and asked, "What did you find, that sent that beast into such a frenzy?"

"I cannot imagine," Sophia answered innocently, contemplating the origin of the ring and the crow's unusual behavior. Albert looked at her suspiciously and urged the horses homeward.

At three, Albert helped Eloise into the cart and drove across the moors to Grimwald to visit with Dagmar. Sophia sat on her bed in her room on the second floor, trying on the newly found jewel. Neither had she seen anything so exquisite, nor had she worn a ring so elegant. It fit perfectly, too perfectly. Her attachment to the ring was instantaneous but her conscience whispered. *This is not a case of finder's keeper's.* It was gorgeous and she adored it. As much as she wanted to believe that it truly belonged to her, her new membership in the McDonnally clan called for resistance. It was not simply a case of possession. She was aware that the ring was valuable and its owner probably searching for it. Wearing it publicly was not an option.

I suppose that I probably *should ask someone about it.*

Chapter VIII

"Fool's Gold"

"We wear the mask
that grins and lies
It hides our cheeks
and shades our eyes"

—Paul Laurence Dunbar

Wednesday afternoon, Sophia sat alone in the parlor waiting for the guests to arrive, occasionally peering out the window in search of an approaching carriage or motorcar. She straightened her skirt, proudly admiring the beautiful fabric. The skirt was one of the many articles, which her uncle, Hiram, purchased for her in London. Sophia felt like a princess from her glittering hairpins, down to her new shoes. Her fingers slid into her skirt pocket to find the ring. After a quick check of the hall, she removed it discreetly and struggled to place it on her *right* ring finger, for the first time. She spread her hand before her, pleased with the sophistication it added to her outfit. The gem sparkled catching the light, streaming through the panes overlooking the drive.

Oh how I wish I could wear it for all to see, she lamented as she attempted to remove it from her finger. The ring would not come off. Her wish, like a tragic ending to a fairytale gone awry, was granted. Sophia pulled and tugged, twisted and turned the ring, but it was determined to remain for all to admire. Sophia began to panic. She tried every possible maneuver, circling the room in her attempts, unaware that her uncle entered the room behind her.

"Sophie?"

Her heart stopped. Nearly out of breath from the ordeal, she thrust her ringed hand into her skirt pocket and turned around to face her uncle, "Uncle...Hiram."

Seeing her flushed face, he rushed over to her. "Sophie, are you ill?"

"No...I," given the opportunity, she jumped in headfirst. "Actually, I am not feeling very well."

It is true, I feel terrible. I am sick with worry, her conscience argued.

"My dear, sit down." He took her left arm and led her to a chair. "You are trembling." Hiram raised his palm to her forehead, "You feel a bit heated."

Sophia looked forlornly; milking her uncle's concern for all that, it was worth. "Yes, Uncle, maybe if I could lie down for a minute," she said pathetically.

"Certainly, love." He positioned the pillow on the settee.

"Not here, the guests will be arriving. Perhaps I could rest in the maid's room for a bit."

"Come, along." He offered her his arm. Hiram slowly escorted Sophia down the hall through the kitchen to the cot in the maid's room. Keeping her right hand lodged in her pocket, she tried to position herself as naturally as possible. Hiram retrieved a gray woolen blanket from the shelf above the cot and covered her gently. "Sophie, I should call Dr. Lambert."

"No, no...I think that I was just nervous about meeting your friend and his sister. I was awfully rude to them, when we were in London."

"You shan't worry about Daniel— not a more forgiving man ever lived. Now, may I get you some water?"

"Some water?"

"Yes, that may help calm you and cool you down."

Hot water will shrink my finger! "On the contrary, I once heard that drinking hot water has a soothing effect."

"Hot water? To drink? Are you sure, Sophia? You look a bit flushed as it is."

"Yes, Uncle, it relaxes, I believe."

"Very well, your wish is my command." Hiram returned to the kitchen and poured a cup of hot water from the kettle on the stove. He offered it to his ailing niece. "Understand that it is still very hot. I will sit it here on the table to cool down.

"Thank you, Uncle; I do not want to detain you. I will be fine."

"I do need to check with Albert about clearing a stall in the stable."

"Go along, I will rest here till the guests arrive."

Hiram nodded and left. Sophia whipped her hand from her pocket and pulled the teacup closer. It was hot, very hot. She grimaced after placing the tip of her index finger in to test the temperature. *I do not have time for it to cool!* She tried again, realizing that the steaming fluid would certainly burn her finger. She brought the cup close to her mouth and began blowing across the surface. She tried inserting a test finger one last time, discovering that she might tolerate it. She slowly slid her ring finger into the cup only to find that the depth was too low.

"Agh! I do not believe this!" She quickly pulled her finger from the cup and thrust it to her side with the sound of approaching footsteps,

Seeing Sophia through the doorway, Naomi inquired, "Sophia, how are you dear? I met your uncle on the way back from the cottage and he informed me that you were feeling poorly."

"Only a little nervous, Aunt Naomi, with the guests and all."

Naomi sat beside Sophia on the cot and took her left hand in hers. Sophia took a sigh of relief that Naomi chose to sit on her left side. Sophia tucked her ringed hand beneath the edge of the blanket.

"Sophia, I have met Daniel, he is a very likeable gentleman. His sister must be very special, as well, for your uncle to invite her for a visit," Naomi added, patting Sophia's hand.

"Thank you, for your concern."

"What is that?" Naomi spotted the steaming cup of water.

"Water. Uncle Hiram brought it for me."

"To drink?"

"Yes."

"I think that tea might be more to your liking, Sophia."

"No, thank you, I am fine now."

"Well, then, I need to speak with Eloise. You rest here until the guests arrive."

"Yes, ma'am."

Naomi left one nervous victim to find the other while Sophia devised a new plan.

I have to get this ring off! I need something to grease it. Oil, where does Eloise keep the oil? She searched the pantry shelves when she eyed a dozen floral molded butter pats on a tray. *Butter? Yes, butter.* She gently lifted one pat off the tray and attempted to slide it around her finger and the band when the butter slipped from her fingers and fell to the floor. Before she had a chance to retrieve it, Naomi's dog, Heidi, was busy licking up the remnants. Eloise entered the kitchen.

"Heidi, you naughty girl!" Eloise scolded. "How did you get that? No biscuits for you today." She looked suspiciously at Sophia. Sophia hid her hand behind her back, cringing with guilt from the reprimand. Sophia shrugged and left the kitchen thinking, *sorry, pup, I will make it up to you later.*

Sophia hurried down the hall and up the staircase to her bedroom. With the less greasy of her two hands, she closed the door behind her. She continued with the struggle to remove the ring, which seemed to be determined to remain on her hand for eternity. She finally wiped her hands and the doorknob with a towel and filled the basin with the pitcher of water. *Cool water. Maybe that will shrink my finger.* She soaked it and soaked it longer, but to no avail. She dried her hands and sat pouting on her bed.

"I wish that I would have left you to be picked up by some other fool."

Eloise Zigmann's features hinted at the beauty that she enjoyed in her youth. Being fifty-five, and not looking a day over forty, she was her husband's pride and joy. Albert took pleasure in showing her off socially, claiming that she was the "finest looking woman this side of the English Channel." Eloise's usual response, "And who would be so beautiful on the other side?"

Today, for the most part, Eloise looked exceptionally well kempt with her uniform starched and perfectly creased. Naomi found Eloise folding napkins in the kitchen. "Eloise, how are you?"

"I am fine, thank you."

"Are you sure?"

"Does it show, Naomi?"

Naomi pointed down to the housekeeper's feet. Eloise looked down following the directing finger. She was mortified to find that in her preoccupation, she inadvertently paired her black right shoe with a brown left one.

"Run back to the cottage and change your shoes, I will cover for you if the guests arrive in your absence. When you return, I shan't leave your side. Try not to worry; I will help you through this."

"Oh, Mum, I am not prepared to meet him. I am a bundle of nerves. Albert will suspect, the moment that he sees Daniel and I together."

"Suspect what, Eloise? There is nothing to suspect. You have not seen that man in twenty years. What is there to suspect?"

"He will see it in my face...Naomi, I am not a liar, and you know that I always tell the truth or something reasonably close to it."

Naomi smiled, knowing Eloise's "honesty" had ironically always given her a great deal of trouble in the past.

"Eloise, direct your attention to Albert when he is present. He will be less suspicious."

"Goodness no, Naomi. If I start giving Albert attention, he will *definitely* know that there is something wrong. It is over, Naomi," Eloise said tearfully. She took a chair by the table. "He will probably challenge Daniel to a dual and Albert will be killed, all because of me," she sniffled.

"Eloise, get a hold of yourself. Think about what you are saying. Albert believes that this is your first meeting with Daniel."

"What if—" Eloise began to speculate.

Hiram poked his head into the kitchen doorway, "Naomi, may I speak with you a minute? Eloise, the guests have arrived."

Naomi nodded encouragingly and followed Hiram into the hall.

"Naomi, could you please, do me a favor?"

"If at all possible, Hiram."

"Daniel's sister, Abigail, is decidedly *difficult*. We have had a few clashes."

"Clashes?"

"Wee ones. I thought you could entertain her…introduce her to the other village women…sew with her or something. I want Daniel's stay to be pleasant, memorable."

"Daniel's? What do you wish for Abigail's?"

Hiram ignored the comment, "Be a good egg, Naomi. Now, I need to check on Sophia."

"I think that she went up to her room, Hiram."

Hiram went upstairs and knocked gently on Sophia's bedroom door. "Sophie, the guests have arrived, do you feel like joining us?"

"Yes, Uncle Hiram, I am feeling much better, thank you." She pulled on a pair of black lace gloves, from the top drawer of the bureau.

"I shan't be a minute."

"Shall I wait for you?"

"No, Uncle, I will come down directly."

"Very well, I will see you downstairs."

Sophia pulled on the gloves, conveniently hiding the belligerent ring from view. She went to the dressing table and pinned a few straggling hairs which had escaped Naomi's styling.

Hiram passed by Eloise in the foyer to wait for the guests in the study. He too was nervous about the arrival. His "challenge" would soon be standing in the portal and he was not wholly confident that he was prepared to meet with her.

Chapter IX

"Mismatch"

"I never saw thee, lovely one,—
Perchance, I never may;
It is not often that we cross
Such people in our way;

But if we meet in distant years,
Or on some foreign shore,
Sure I can take my Bible oath
I've seen that face before."

—Oliver Wendell Holmes

The O'Leardon carriage halted at the manor, on schedule that afternoon. The magnificence of the mansion overwhelmed the two guests.

"Abby, hae ya e'r seen a more lovely estate? It is as large and handsome as its master."

"The estate is impressive enough," Abigail agreed without further comment on its owner. The O'Leardons left the carriage and approached the main door.

After a minute of deliberation, Hiram left the study and moved to the parlor with Naomi. Naomi watched sympathetically while Eloise performed the "death march" to the door with the drumming of the doorknocker. "Chin up!" she called to the bewildered housekeeper. Hiram raised his brows in confusion.

Eloise unlatched the door, when Albert appeared behind her. She prayed that he would still be her husband by the end of the day.

"Welcome, Mr. and Miss O'Leardon," Eloise greeted softly.

Daniel's face lit up like a Christmas tree the moment that he saw Eloise. "Hello, hello," he said slowly, not believing his eyes. "Ah, yes...this is me sister, Abigail O'Leardon."

"My pleasure, ma'am. Will you please come in? Albert will get your bags."

Albert wondered curiously, as to why the gentleman did not introduce himself properly to his wife. He removed their luggage from the carriage to take them inside and paused in the portal when he saw Daniel, now in the hall, take Eloise's hand in his.

"Your beauty is like summer in Ireland."

Eloise was lost in Daniel's gaze. Albert considered blurring it.

"Better keep an eye on my brother; he is quite a man with the ladies." Abigail alerted Eloise. Eloise held her breath and Naomi tensed up, knowing Albert's character.

Albert paused, mentally defying Daniel to make one more move toward his wife, then asked, "Eloise, which rooms?" he said gruffly.

"The two at the end of the hall on the left. The first being Miss O'Leardon, the second being Dan— Mr. O'Leardon's."

Albert narrowed his eyes with his wife's near miss with the name and left reluctantly to carry the bags upstairs.

Eloise was frozen until Hiram called and suggested that she take the guests coats and escort them into the parlor. She did so and Hiram and Naomi welcomed the O'Leardons, inviting them to sit. The manor's master and Abigail temporary locked stares, unsure as to the other's thoughts. Abigail removed her hat and sat it on the table next to her, avoiding any acknowledgement that Hiram had sat down next to her. Sophia then appeared in the archway. Daniel and Hiram rose with her arrival. She was the epitome of the beauty of youth and grace, with one exception: the black lace gloves with the pastel-colored apparel.

All eyes were on Sophia's hands. Blushing, she announced, "Hello, everyone, I am Sophia McDonnally...and the gloves?" She held at her hands proudly, "They were a 'going away' gift from my mother."

Abigail left her chair immediately to take a better look. "They are absolutely elegant, Sophia. I am Abigail O'Leardon, Daniel's sister." Her introduction left Hiram feeling negligent of his duty as host.

"My pleasure, Miss O'Leardon." Sophia immediately sensed that she had gained an ally and entered comfortably alongside Abigail. "My uncle has spoken highly of you."

Abigail squinted suspiciously at Hiram. "Highly, you say?" then resumed her position in the chair next to his.

Hiram continued with the proper introductions and took his place next to Abigail. He informed Daniel and Abigail of Edward's mishap and then asked Eloise to bring in the refreshments. Eloise, relieved to leave the room *and* Daniel, was leery of returning with a loaded serving tray. Naomi watched her wilting friend leave.

In the hall, out of sight, Eloise paused, closed her eyes and took a few deep breaths.

"A man with the ladies, indeed," Albert, having returned to the hall, echoed behind her.

Eloise's eyes flashed open fearfully. "Not really," she spoke softly with feelings of guilt for the falsehood. She then scurried for the kitchen.

Worried about her friend and Eloise's return, Naomi decided to assist. "If you will excuse me, I will give Eloise a hand with the trays."

Hiram nodded and all returned to their seats.

"Why on God's green earth would ya stay in that wee flat in town when ya have a home as beautiful as this?" Daniel asked.

"Why Daniel, is it not obvious? To visit my dearest friend."

Daniel smiled approvingly but Abigail looked skeptically. In the archway, Albert steamed, cleared his throat and sent a contemptuous glance in Daniel's direction.

"Yes, Albert?" Hiram inquired.

"Sir, shall I put the horses and the carriage in the stable for the night?"

"Yes, I think that Daniel and his sister have traveled quite long enough for one day."

"Yes, sir." Albert left with one last threatening stare to Daniel.

Hiram found his caretaker's behavior unexpected and unacceptable. "Pardon me for asking Daniel, but were you formally acquainted with Mr. Zigmann?"

"No, Hiram."

"I will speak to him. My apologies, I am truly embarrassed."

"Think nothin' o' it, Hiram. Please dunna say anythin' to ya caretaker, 'twas only a wee misunderstanding," Daniel reassured knowing his liberal behavior with Eloise had unintentionally instigated Albert's negativity.

"Very well, but please inform me if he acts with any further disrespect," Hiram insisted.

Abigail found Hiram's interest in her brother's welfare to be admirable, being her first positive thought to Mr. McDonnally's character.

Eloise and Naomi entered the parlor carrying the two silver trays, heavy with tea and crumpets. Eloise's hands trembled as she sat the tray on the only vacant table, which was inconveniently located next to Daniel's chair. "Relax, Ellie," Daniel whispered trying to comfort her. Eloise refused to face the freckled countenance, backed away and asked her employer to be excused.

"Yes, you may go now. The trays are beautiful. Thank you, Eloise."

"Thank you, sir." Eloise, with her face of stone, took little time in exiting to the kitchen. Once there, she paused, remembering Daniel's sweet words of comfort. She closed her eyes, once again. *Oh God, I am truly sorry for failing the test. Freckleswept again...and in the master's house.* Her thoughts were broken when Naomi's dachsie, Heidi, closed in the maid's room for temporary safe-keeping, began to whimper.

"Oh, do you need to go out, Heidi?" Eloise cracked the door open. She bent down to pick up the little dog when Heidi shot past her fingers and made a beeline for the parlor.

"Wait! No, Heidi! Come back!" she called, chasing after her, down the hall.

Heidi sped into the parlor, directly to the guests, growling and barking wildly. Abigail shrieked and jumped to her feet and flew into the closest available arms, Hiram's. Naturally, everyone responded simultaneously, adding more chaos to the situation.

"Stop it, Heidi!" Naomi demanded.

"Come here, girl!" Sophia begged

"I am so sorry, Master McDonnally," Eloise pleaded, feeling dimwitted.

"Y'er all right, Abby," Daniel said, comforting his sister.

Hiram was silent for a moment basking in the pleasure of the close encounter with his very attractive, yet hostile guest. Finally, when the commotion failed to cease, with one protective arm around Abigail he motioned with the other and demanded, "Someone please get the dog out of here!"

Sophia seized the wriggling pup and carried it off to the kitchen. Abigail lifted her head at the silence, still shaken from the intrusion. She immediately moved away from her host's embrace.

"I beg your pardon. It was so unexpected, I...if you do not mind, I will step outside for a minute for some air."

"I will accompany you, Miss O'Leardon," Naomi offered.

"No, please stay here and enjoy the tea," Abigail insisted as she left the room.

"She will be fine; she was attacked by a dog when she was a wee lass. She has always been a bit fearful, since then," Daniel explained.

Hiram immediately excused himself to find Abigail, retrieving her coat from the hall rack.

Eloise apologized profusely, barely holding back the tears. She dropped her head, saw the mismatched shoes on her feet, panicked and fled to the hall. Daniel watched feeling more sympathy for the little housekeeper, love of his past, than his sister.

Hiram found Abigail gazing across the moors, standing on the opposite side of the drive. He placed her coat over her shoulders. "My apologies."

Abigail turned in surprise to see Hiram standing beside her. "You need not be embarrassed, Miss O'Leardon."

"I am not! I was taken by surprise, that is all."

"Perhaps an occasional short walk with Naomi's dog would defuse your fears. I could join you," he offered generously.

"I dare say that Mrs. McDonnally is quite capable of walking her own dog. If I so choose to take the dog for a walk, I assure you that I am not a child and not in need of your assistance. Shall we return to the house?" Abigail snapped.

"Yes, I *think that we should*," Hiram agreed, irritated with Abigail's continuing belligerence and ungrateful attitude.

When they returned to the parlor, Daniel was informing Naomi of his latest acquisitions at the bookstore while she expressed a particular interest in the Sherlock Holmes mysteries. Sophia returned and took a seat in the over-stuffed chair, happy to be back with the guests and the refreshments. Daniel lifted the tray and presented it to her. She started to reach for a biscuit when Hiram reminded her, "Sophia, I think perhaps you may want to remove your gloves before you enjoy the sweets. After all, you were carrying the dog."

"You are quite right, Uncle," she agreed and removed the right glove when she realized her mistake. Abigail immediately commented on the extravagant ring.

"My, Sophia, what an extraordinary, beautiful piece. Did your mother give that to you, as well?"

Sophia's mind raced, seeking an explanation when Naomi asked, "Yes, Sophia, *who* gave you that ring?" Naomi shocked to see the ring, which she believed to be in Harriet Dugan's possession.

For lack of a more creative response, Sophia went with the familiar, "My friend, Guillaume, gave it to me."

Hiram, who was equally surprised at the size and quality of Sophia's ring, asked, "*Guillaume?*"

"We have been friends for years. I knew him in Paris," Sophia explained weakly.

"Indeed, what a dear friend he must be," Abigail smiled.

Hiram and Naomi looked suspiciously at one another. Neither felt comfortable with suspecting Sophia's credibility, but felt that they had no other choice, for the time being.

Daniel sensed the tension surrounding the ring and changed the subject. "Hiram, a new book came in 'bout the *Wasp*, the motor car that won the International 500 Mile Sweepstakes Race."

Naomi could not take her eyes off the ring. Daniel noticed Naomi's preoccupation and Sophia's discomfort and brought Naomi into the con-versation, next. "Did ya hear about the race, Naomi? It was in May a few years back."

"Yes, Daniel...an American driver, yes, it was an American who took first place. The purse was, I believe, ten thousand dollars."

Hiram joined in, still disturbed by his confrontation with Abigail in the drive. "Yes, it was a chap by the name of Harroun. There was some controversy about the winner— another driver believed that he had been cheated and *treated unfairly.*" Hiram turned and glared at Abigail.

Sophia quickly interjected, "How long did it take them to drive the five hundred miles, Mr. O'Leardon?"

"No need to be formal. *Daniel* would be fine. O'er six hours, they were travelin' almost seventy-five miles per hour," Daniel confirmed.

"That is awfully fast and dangerous. Was there not someone killed during the race, Hiram?" Naomi asked the obviously disturbed host.

"Aye, in the eleventh lap, 'twas not the driver, 'twas his *innocent* riding mechanic," Hiram turned once again to Abigail with his dark eyes blazing.

"Hiram, the *Wasp* had a rear view mirror, did it not?" Naomi asked nervously, her glance flitting to Hiram, to Abigail, and back to him.

"Yes, *he* had the advantage over the others, with the ability *to see what was coming.*" His gaze toward Abigail, neither faltered, nor lost its intensity. Sophia viewed her uncle's behavior with shocked curiosity.

Abigail shifted and defensively changed the subject, "I prefer horse and buggy, myself. Our cousin Rupert attended the American race in ought six when Dan Patch broke the world record for the mile," she reported proudly.

"Aye, what a horse. Me cousin said the crowd went wild, and that horse just turned its head to the cheerin' crowd like it knew what it had done. I wish I coulda been there and seen it for meself. Unbelievable," Daniel exclaimed.

"Yes, *unbelievable*," Hiram glowered at Abigail.

Fed up with Hiram's running commentary, Daniel's sister made an attempt to escape. "Although the conversation is stimulating, the trip was lengthy and I thought that if it would not be too much of an inconvenience, I might take a short nap before dinner."

"I will take you to your room, Abigail. Eloise appears to be indisposed temporarily," Naomi offered with relief, aware of Hiram's volatile temper.

"Thank you. Sophia, Daniel." Abigail gave a sideways glance to the host and mumbled, "Mr. McDonnally, I will see you at dinner."

"Yes, you will, Miss O'Leardon."

With his severe tone, Sophia nervously bit her bottom lip.

As they approached the stairs, Naomi informed Abigail, "You have the room next to Sophia's. I think that you will find it very agreeable."

"Naomi, might I ask you a question?" Abigail asked as they reached the last step to the second floor.

"Certainly."

"How does anyone tolerate, Mr. McDonnally's attitude?"Abigail said spitefully.

"Abigail, he is a very generous and under-standing man. But, mind you, he is strong-willed and no one knows, better than I that his temper is not to be trifled with."

"I am not intimidated in the least."

"I shan't pretend that I did not notice a rift between the two of you, nor do I expect to be privy to your conflict with Hiram. However, I must caution you, he has suffered a great deal in his lifetime. His losses are great. It could be a long arduous journey back into his good graces, once you have fallen from them. It might behoove you to humor him while enjoying his hospitality," Naomi suggested and opened the door to a beautifully decorated room in olive green and gold.

"This room is quite elegant, Naomi. Are you and Sophia the only other occupants in this incredible mansion?"

"No, my daughter Allison is staying here with me until the wedding. Then we will move to Brachney Hall with Edward."

Abigail ran her hand across the satin pillow on the chair. "Do you speak of Hiram, with experience?"

"When one is young, love is new and difficult to cope with. If you need anything, just ring." The word "ring" immediately took Naomi back to the disturbing situation with Sophia, but then she continued. "I am anxious for you to meet, Edward, and our daughter Allison."

"Yes, I was sorry to hear about the accident."

"We appreciate your concern. I will knock just before dinner."

"Thank you, Naomi, and thank you for the information."

Naomi smiled, "You can never have too much information, especially in this case," Naomi concurred and left feeling certain this would not be the last skirmish between Hiram and the hot-tempered redhead.

However, Naomi *was* uncomfortably indecisive about the best alternative in handling the situation with Sophia and the ring. Naomi knew that Hiram had no way of knowing that the ring belonged to Mrs. Dugan and questioned as to whether or not she should inform him. She was torn, having seen Harriet Dugan donning a different ring from her husband, Joseph, at the Burns' Night celebration.

Perhaps, Harriet lost the other ring. Guillaume found it and did give it to Sophia, exactly as she said.

Naomi eventually resolved to be blindly content with this deduction, giving Sophia the benefit of the doubt.

Chapter X

"The Ribbon"

"I had a dream— a strange, wild dream—
Said a dear voice at early light;
And even yet its shadows seem
To linger in my waking sight."

—William Bryant

Abigail walked over to the bedroom window and looked out over the grounds where her adversary was strolling leisurely through the garden with her brother.

Hiram McDonnally, you despicable, disagreeable man... yet so pleasing to the eye, she thought with agitation. She unbuttoned her jacket, hung it over a chair, and lay down on the bed, staring up at the ceiling.

"I am no fool; I will not fall for you, Hiram McDonnally, you, nor any other wealthy scoundrel." Abigail turned her head, closed her eyes and fell into a deep sleep, dreaming of her recent encounter.

"Miss O'Leardon, this is my new motorcar, the Wasp. *Shall we take a ride across the moors?"*

"No thank you, Mr. McDonnally. I would rather stay and have tea with Naomi."

"Does it not meet your standards? I paid a handsome price for it. Ten-thousand American dollars."

"I prefer horse and buggy, Mr. McDonnally."

"Look, Eloise is letting the dog out, you better get in the car quickly, Miss O'Leardon!"

"Hurry! Open the door, I am afraid!"

Hiram pulled her into the car and started the engine.

"Where are we going, Hiram? You are driving too fast! "

Hiram threw back his head and laughed. "Only seventy-five miles per hour, Miss O'Leardon. We will be late for the race."

Abigail woke up with a start. She looked around the room, relieved to find that she had only been dreaming and fell back to sleep.

While she slept, Daniel felt the necessity to question his friend about the ongoing discordance with his sister.

"Hiram, what has Abby done now?"

"Daniel, for the life of me, I cannot understand, nor predict your sister's behavior. Her animosity towards me seems to be growing minute to minute, despite my congenial actions. I can only imagine that her only motive for accepting my invitation was to feed her obsession with tormenting me."

"Hiram, that is just her way. Abby speaks her mind."

"I support women who are self-sufficient and independent, but her attitude towards me is abominable." Hiram closed his eyes, *Yet, I am so taken with her.* He looked to his friend, confounded and weary. "Does she display this outrageous behavior with everyone she meets?"

"Hiram, for reasons that I am not at liberty to discuss, wit' a promise on me word o' honor, me sister has what ya might call a personal vendetta against the men o' the world. Excludin' meself, most o' the time. I would not blame ya if ya n'er spoke to me sister agin, but she is a good soul. I ask ya as a friend, dun't give up on her." Daniel took a seat on the concrete bench. "But, if ya choose, I *will* be takin' her home."

"No, no..." Hiram began to pace, "that would be too simple for her." He ran his fingers through his hair. "Contrary to her beliefs, I *am not* to be punished for another man's mistakes. No, this time I am not walking away, Daniel. First Naomi and then Elizabeth. My friend, if your sister thinks that I will not stand up to her, she is in for a very enlightening visit."

Daniel questioned Hiram's motives and shuddered with the thought of the transformation of his sister and best friend into two very capable opponents preparing for battle.

Hiram's pacing became more deliberate. "Begging your pardon, but your sister will be the last woman to walk away from me without a proper explanation." With this blatant conviction, Daniel looked aghast.

"Hiram—"

"Daniel, you need not worry. I intend to be hospitable enough and civil to Abigail. However, given the opportunity, I will confront her privately if she continues to berate me. Daniel, you would not tolerate this either."

"Agreed, my friend, but are the battle scars wort' yer efforts?"

"There is no point engaging in war, if you do not intend to win."

Daniel made no additional comments.

After a short, quiet walk along the pathways, Daniel asked, "Would that be the caretakers' cottage?"

"Yes, Mr. and Mrs. Zigmann live there. Their son, Guillaume, is visiting, but as you know, staying at my uncle's home, Brachney Hall."

"Aye. Hiram, how long have ya known the Zigmanns?"

"Not long, a few months, but they have been taking care of the estate for years. Edward hired them when I was in Switzerland. Why do you ask?"

"No particular reason." Silence reigned.

"Daniel? I have known you long enough to detect when you have something bothering you." Hiram realized his friend was not going to expand. "Is it Albert?"

"No, no, 'tis not Albert... his wife, Eloise. 'Tis very difficult for her. Ellie has many duties," Daniel commented with concern. Hiram stopped by the pasture gate. *Ellie?* Hiram looked suspiciously at Daniel's concerned face.

"Daniel, you need not worry about Eloise. I do very little entertaining. She may be a wee bit nervous, but Naomi will assist her." He patted his friend's back, thinking it somewhat odd that Daniel was preoccupied with his housekeeper and continued, pointing out the perimeter of the estate.

Abigail lay curled on the bed in the guest room and drifted off, experiencing yet another dream.

"Miss O'Leardon, would you care to join me to walk the dog after dinner?"

"Very well, Mr. McDonnally, I will get my coat and the new black gloves that Sophia gave me."

Heidi began growling ferociously and Hiram rushed to Abigail's side.

"Eloise, get a leash on that beast and get it out of here!"

"Yes, Master McDonnally." *Hiram smiled and took Abigail's arm in his.*

"Come, let us go for a walk, Abigail, I will give you a tour of my estate."

"It is beautiful, Mr. McDonnally."

"Please call me, Hyatt."

"Hyatt? No, that is not your name. What is it?"

"Fear not, you may call me Master McDonnally. Someday, you will live here too. We will all live together."

"Are you sure that this is what you want, Master McDonnally?"

"Naturally, I cannot imagine my life without you and Daniel." He flashed Sophia's ring before her eyes.

"Oh, sir…"Abigail sighed.

"Yes, the Zigmanns will move to Brachney Hall to work for Edward, so as to make the cottage available for you and your brother."

"The cottage?"

"Yes, your brother loves working out of doors and you my dear, would look splendid in black and white, serving my meals."

"Aghh!" Abigail woke, breathing hard, and having difficulty distinguishing between the nightmare and reality. She sat up and reviewed the short memory of her dream. Naomi's knocking gave her no choice but to abandon her negative thoughts and prepare for dinner.

"It is time for dinner, Abigail."

"Thank you, Naomi," Abigail called back. Naomi returned to the kitchen to have Eloise prepare a second basket for Edward. The first, covered with a linen cloth, would be delivered to Allison and Guillaume, dining at the cottage with Albert.

Abigail washed, combed her hair, powdered her face and put on her jacket before facing the others for dinner. She went downstairs and found Eloise bustling about the dining room. The alcohol burner was percolating the coffee, an oddity in a household of tea drinkers. Eloise had prepared Mrs. O'Hara's Irish stew recipe in honor of the guests and was doing her best to serve without spilling the filled bowls.

Hiram took his usual place at the table with Naomi on his left, leaving a vacant chair on his right for Daniel, next to his sister. Naomi took her position when Sophia arrived and pleaded for Daniel to sit next to her to facilitate their discussion about Paris. This left only one alternative for Abigail— to take the only other available chair, which Hiram graciously pulled out for her. Sitting on Hiram's right was too close for comfort, for obvious reasons.

Hiram said grace and then while passing the bread he turned to Abigail. "Did you sleep well?"

Both Abigail and Hiram looked puzzled for a minute with an instance of deja vous, which they recognized as originating at *The Crystal Cup* that morning after they met. Abigail struggled with the truth about the nature of her nap, then nodded, "Yes, thank you."

"Perhaps after dinner, you would like to go for a walk, Miss O'Leardon. I will show you the estate," Hiram asked in his most hospitable voice. Abigail could not believe her ears, her dream revisited. But she soon realized it not to be an unusual request.

"Ya would enjoy it, Abby. Hiram gave me the grand tour while ya were restin'."

"That would be fine," Abigail agreed with little emotion.

"Capital," Hiram smiled, feeling that he had won the first round. Abigail, on the other hand, knew that she had stepped into the ring with an opponent twice her size, which signaled her defenses to take guard.

"Miss O'Leardon, might I inquire as to why you do not share your brother's delightful accent?" Hiram asked in passing.

"Mr. McDonnally, do you make a habit of insulting your guests, before even the soup is served!"

Abigail threw down her napkin and marched out of the dining room to return to her bedroom. Daniel smacked his forehead with frustration, Sophia and Naomi sat in awe, motionless, while the offender quickly excused himself. Hiram's long stride delivered him in little time to the bottom of the steps to block the peeved woman from continuing to her room.

"Miss O'Leardon, please return to the dining room. I apologize, if you overreacted to my comment," he said with as much diplomacy as possible.

"*Overreacted?* You delighted in insulting me in the presence of a room full of strangers and *I* overreacted?" she scorned.

"A room full of strangers? Three people besides me and one of those was your brother! You are being far too sensitive, Miss O'Leardon," Hiram said condescendingly.

"Now, I am too sensitive! Any more negative comments that you would like to make before I leave?"

"Aye, you are far too beautiful to dine alone upstairs, pouting in your room. Would you not have greater pleasure, making me miserable at my own table?" He folded his arms across his chest.

Abigail's appetite for the challenge and the delicious meal dictated her next move— to rejoin the other guests. Hiram strolled behind her with his hands clasped behind his back with an expression resembling that of the cat that swallowed the canary.

During their absence, Sophia and Daniel's discussion of their Paris memoirs continued, making Eloise extremely ill at ease, Paris being the location of her last meeting with Daniel. She excused herself to prepare the dessert, but on returning, Hiram requested that it be served later in the evening. Heidi's barking in the kitchen gave the housekeeper another opportunity to escape Daniel's sweet smile. Daniel's continued attentiveness to his employee, gave cause for Hiram's disquieting concern.

After the meal, Sophia and Naomi delivered the basket to Edward at Brachney Hall. Daniel chose to stay behind and carried his cup of coffee to the kitchen. Hiram sat alone with Abigail, whose hostility had gone into temporary hibernation while she fortified her commentary garrisons for the walk.

"Shall we take a turn around the estate?" Hiram cheerily invited.

Abigail nodded and Hiram escorted her to the hall and assisted the stoic woman with her coat.

"I will show you the garden first, Miss O'Leardon, however, very little is in bloom yet."

Abigail followed, somewhat unnerved with the thought that she was going to be alone with him and his accommodating attitude.

Daniel joined Eloise in the kitchen.

"Hello, Ellie."

"Daniel?" Eloise looked up in surprise.

"May I sit with ya and talk a bit?"

"I am awfully busy, Mr. O'Leardon. I need to clear the table." Eloise chose an empty tray from the pantry with fearful thoughts that Albert may find them together.

"After twenty years, do ya think a few minutes would be too much to ask of ya?"

Caught off guard with his candor, Eloise replied, embarrassed, "No, can I get you some more coffee?"

"No thank ya, Ellie."

In passing the kitchen, Hiram observed Daniel speaking quietly with Eloise. Hiram paused, as did Abigail, and then continued, opening the backdoor for his guest.

Daniel and Eloise? They both thought.

Eloise and Daniel sat down across from each other at the table, neither knowing how the conversation would evolve.

"How have you been, Daniel?"

"Lonely...I ne'r married...I ne'er forgot about ya, Ellie. I ne'er should have left ya and gone back to Ireland. Me regrets do not change the facts, they are o' no consequence now."

Eloise's mouth opened to speak, but the words would not come. There were no words to express the shock of his confession. Eloise swallowed, incapable of taking her eyes from his.

"How is your son, Guillaume, Ellie?"

"Guillaume? He is on the mend. You will meet him Friday night at Brachney Hall," Eloise said in a monotone, still reeling from Daniel's statement.

"Will ya be attendin', Ellie?"

"NO!" she left her chair and walked to the window. "I mean, yes. Albert and I have been invited," she retracted. "Daniel, I never told Albert," Eloise turned wringing her hands.

"About us, Ellie?" Daniel stood up.

"Daniel, Albert is a very jealous man," she said fearfully.

"A wee bit o' jealousy is good for a man. Makes a man appreciate his wife. Is he a good man, Ellie? Does he treat you well?"

"Albert is a wonderful man. He has been very good to us, Guillaume and me."

Daniel pulled a leather wallet from his inner jacket pocket. He opened it slowly. Eloise watched curiously. His large fingers trembled slightly as he lifted out an ivory lace ribbon and laid it on the table.

Eloise looked at it, and then looked up with questioning eyes.

"It is yers, Ellie. Remember, you gave it to me that first year. We were at the park and I was in need o' a bookmark." He picked up and slid it through his fingers. "Ya pulled it from yer hair. Do ya remember?"

Eloise stared at the ribbon in disbelief.

"Surprised, Ellie? It has been right here, e'r since that day...I had it wi' me that day at the train station, in Paris. I wanted to show ya, then... but ya spent the hours speakin' o' yer baby son and yer husband. Happy, ya were. I ne'er doubted that they were yer entire world."

Eloise felt that she was in some strange dream as she listened to Daniel's tender words. Daniel folded the ribbon and replaced it reverently for safekeeping. Looking at the wallet, he explained with some difficulty.

"Ellie... I am only showin' this to ya now cause... cause I need ya to know that I bring no trouble for yer family." He spoke with deep sincerity as he faced her. Eloise felt his pain as her eyes welled up with sympathetic tears.

"Ellie, if there e'r comes a day when ya are lonely and the happiness has vanished from yer life..." He replaced the wallet to his pocket, "Ya will find me in London."

A broad smile spread across Daniel's freckled face. He handed Eloise the empty tray, "I have kept ya from yer duties long enough. Good evenin', Ellie." Daniel left the kitchen.

The somber face of Mrs. Albert Zigmann stared down at the empty tray as a single tear fell to it.

Chapter XI

"Fighting Fire with Fire"

"She listened with
a flitting blush
With downcast eyes
and modest grace;
For well she knew
I could not choose
To look upon her face."

—Samuel T. Coleridge

Hiram and Abigail spent several minutes in the garden while Hiram proudly expanded on his improvement plans with his anticipation of the returning perennials.

"I *am* astonished to find the magnificent Master of McDonnally Manor showing an interest in something as trivial as flowers," Abigail said sarcastically.

"I assure you Miss O'Leardon that I have a very special interest in God's miracles which cleverly conceal their potential beauty," Hiram defended keenly.

Abigail studied his dark eyes dancing mischievously and then escaped them pointing to the horses in the distance. "Are those yours?"

"No, they are Edward's prize possessions. We share the pasture. Couple of large lads, a Percheron and the white Hannoverian."

"Percheron? That is an enormous horse."

"Aye, Hunter is all of seventeen hands, but not too large for Edward. He rides it as if it were a pony."

"Is your uncle a very large man?"

"Edward, large?" He laughed, "No, an average chap, but his heart is bigger than any man's. That is the caretaker's cottage, but I guess you assumed as much. Someday, you and Daniel—"

Abigail's heart stopped. Before she had a chance to draw any similarities to her earlier dream, the neighbor, Mrs. Dugan appeared scurrying through the fields, yelling between breaths.

"Master McDonnally, help me, me shed's on fire! I canna put it out!"

Hiram glanced to the sky above the trees dividing the properties to see a stream of black smoke snaking upward. He opened the gate to the pasture and called out, "Mrs. Dugan, I am on my way! Wait here," he instructed Abigail. "Where is Joseph?" he asked running toward Harriet.

"He has gone to the village," she said, short of breath.

The two ran toward the Dugan shed when Abigail called to them, "Wait, I can help!" She opened the gate and took out after them.

The three arrived on the scene to find smoke pouring out of the opened window of the shed. Hiram pulled off his jacket, put his handkerchief over his nose and mouth and ran inside.

"Be careful, Hiram!" Abigail shrieked.

The two women immediately began filling the buckets from the well and passing them into Hiram. The fire, although confined to a small area spread to the corner of the shed. Hiram quickly moved a number of tools out of harm's way and then continued dousing the fire until it smoldered and the smoke dissipated. He stood inside exhasted, examining the damage when he heard Abigail calling.

"Hiram, Hiram, are you all right?"

Her concerned voice was music to his ears. *So the woman cares, does she?* He ran his blackened fingers down his beard. He smiled with yet another victory and decided another minute within the barn would definitely be to his advantage.

"Hiram, Hiram!" Abigail called desperately.

Covered in soot and sweat and looking worse than he felt, he walked to the shed doorway. There he was met with Abigail's grateful embrace.

"I thought that you..." she said with teary-eyed relief.

Hiram smiled down at her and took the opportunity to run his fingers through her fallen tresses, realizing that Abigail was indeed a *Spring Spirit*. Abigail pulled back objectionably.

"I was concerned for my brother, you *are* his friend," she denounced, embarrassed that she exhibited feelings which she had been struggling to suppress.

Mrs. Dugan raised her eyebrows in doubt to the young woman's less than believable explanation and then assisted the looming, rejected hero over to a bench at the side of the house. She offered him a dipper of water and sang his praises for a job well done. "Master McDonnally, I canna thank ye enough. Come in the house, you will be gettin' a chill," Harriet insisted.

"Mrs. Dugan, I do not think that you want the likes of me in your home." Hiram motioned to his filthy condition.

"Ne'er ye mind, one's always honored to hae a McDonnally make a call." She offered to help him from the bench and into the house. In the cottage, Harriet Dugan, nearly sixty, yet spry on her stout legs, hurried about the kitchen, heating water and retrieving cloths. She offered a cloth to Abigail who sat down, unsuccessfully removing the dirt and soot from her dress, reminders of her loss of control. Hiram watched with amusement and motioned to the frustrated young woman.

"Mrs. Dugan, may I present Abigail O'Leardon, my friend Daniel's sister."

"Me pleasure, miss." *O'Leardon?*

"Mine, I am sure, Mrs. Dugan," Abigail nodded and smiled uncomfortably, self-conscious of her disheveled appearance.

"Strange way to be meetin', but I thank ye

kindly for yer help, Miss O'Connor." Abigail immediately looked to Hiram.

"*Miss O'Leardon*, Mrs. Dugan," Hiram gently corrected, then glanced at Abigail.

"Aye, that would be the other...if it wouldna be much trouble, lassie, could ye fetch the towels on the line out back?" Abigail left out the back door, giving herself a mental thrashing for falling prey to Hiram's charms.

"She is verra beautiful, Mr. McDonnally. Convenient 'avin' a friend with such a bonny lass for a sister, ay?"

"Aye, Mrs. Dugan," Hiram winked at Harriet.

"Aye, but she is a wee bit flighty. O' course, the Irish canna help theyselves."

Hiram grinned with the undeniable truth in her words. Harriet dipped a cloth in the pan of warm water, wiped her champion's face, and asked, "Who would be her brother?"

"Daniel O'Leardon," Hiram reaffirmed.

Daniel, Daniel O'Leardon? Could it be the same? "Not Eloise's Daniel?" Harriet inquired with surprise when her husband, Joseph, entered the cottage. The sight of his wife with Hiram sent him storming to the kitchen.

"What goes on here, woman?"

Hiram jumped to his feet with the resounding roar of Joseph's voice. Fortunately, Abigail entered the backdoor with the towels, diffusing Joseph's anger with the assumption of any questionable behavior between Mr. McDonnally and his wife.

"Hello, Mr. Dugan, this is Miss O'Leardon. I—" Hiram began.

"He saved yer shed, that 'tis what he did!" Harriet slammed the pot to the stove.

"Me shed?" Joseph ran to peer out the backdoor.

"Caught fire, ye wouldna listen to me, I canna tell ye how many times I warned ye 'bout that moldin' hay!" Harriet scolded.

Joseph ran out back to survey the damage to his beloved tool shed. Hiram joined him shortly thereafter. "Sorry, Mr. Dugan."

"I should be thankin' ye that it wasna a total loss." Joseph extended his hand in gratitude.

Hiram shook it, "I have a number of boards in the barn left from the raising of our shed. They are yours, if you need them."

"No, thank ye, I wouldna be needin' charity."

"'tis a shame, to use it for firewood," Hiram said skillfully.

"If that be the case, I guess I will be takin' it off yer hands. No sense havin' it go to waste," Joseph proudly answered. "Jock is hitched up out front, if ye and the lassie would be needin' a ride back," Joseph offered.

Abigail stood in the doorway admiring Hiram for his unwavering generosity, but said nothing. Mrs. Dugan observed, "He is quite a man, ye canna deny it."

Abigail turned, "I suppose, if you like that type."

"Are ye blind lassie?" Harriet mumbled under her breath.

"Pardon me, Mrs. Dugan?"

"Here's a basket of biscuits for ye to be takin'," Harriet handed Abigail a small woven basket covered with a tartan cloth. "Not verra much of a thank ye for all ye did."

"Thank you, Mrs. Dugan." Abigail smiled gratefully.

"Lassie, ye willna come across too many men agreeable as the handsome Mr. McDonnally," Harriet promoted. Abigail dare not contradict the endorsement, out of sheer respect for Mrs. Dugan. She held her tongue and smiled gratefully.

Joseph and Hiram returned to inform Abigail that they were ready to leave. The three climbed into the cart. Harriet stood on the stoop waving her handkerchief, miffed, thinking, *Me dearest friend in the world and she didna tell me that she invited Daniel O'Leardon? I hae a mind to ne'er speak to her again.*

"What must Albert be thinking? Ohh...I will be payin' me friend a visit verra soon," Harriet nodded as the cart began the short journey to the estate.

Angel, the Dugan's dachsie awoke in the back, climbed up, and from behind, nudged Abigail. Abigail let out a short shriek. Seeing the unwelcome dog on her left, she edged toward the lesser of two evils, Hiram, on her right. With this pleasant maneuver, Hiram immediately snagged the opportunity and enclosed his arm around her. The moment Abigail was prepared to express her disapproval; the cart hit a rut in the road nearly throwing her from her seat, saved only by Hiram's clutch. She refrained from complaint and temporarily surrendered, while they drove in the drifting light of the sunset.

Eloise's Daniel? Hiram thought uneasily.

The little cart continued toward the manor when it came upon a large white figure along the side of the road.

"Look, a horse! It looks like your uncle's," Abigail sat up with surprise.

"It *is*. I cannot imagine how it escaped from the pasture...Can you Miss O'Leardon?" Hiram looked down reproachfully at Abigail, under his arm.

"Oh..." Abigail sank down in the seat.

She lowered her head in shame for leaving the pasture gate ajar. Hiram shook his head and turned away to conceal his smile from the guilty party. When they reached the spot where the escapee grazed, Hiram called out, "C'mon Duff!" The horse raised its head and trotted gracefully behind the cart.

"Well-trained," Joseph remarked.

"Aye, more so than some people," Hiram grinned, giving Abigail a slight squeeze within his arm. Abigail's self-esteem suffered considerable damage and feared that the other horse may be running free, as well. At the estate, Albert met the cart, "Hunter chose to stay and enjoy the oats," he reported. Abigail gave a sigh of relief.

"Glad to hear it. Please help Joseph load the extra lumber that we have in the barn. He will be using it to make a few repairs," Hiram instructed.

"Yes, sir."

Albert led the runaway back to the barn. Hiram helped Abigail down from the cart and escorted her into the house. Abigail remained quiet and followed Eloise. Eloise drew her bath while Hiram searched for Daniel, who he found reading alone in the parlor. Upon seeing his less than immaculate friend within the archway, Daniel closed the volume and stood.

"Hiram, ol' man, what in the world have ya been doin'? Cleanin' the flues?"

"There was a small fire in the neighbor's shed."

"Is everyone all right?"

"Yes, the damage was minimal...Daniel, I must insist that you convey the nature of the relationship which you share with my housekeeper."

This was the last question, Daniel expected. He resumed his position and opened the book. "Hiram, do not trouble yerself with me affairs," Daniel said sternly.

Hiram stood his ground, "Daniel, I welcome you here as my brother, but I will not allow my household to be disrupted."

Daniel lowered the novel to his lap and explained. "Ellie... Mrs. Zigmann and I were together when I was but one and twenty. I returned home to Ireland, Ellie stayed in Germany and married. Years later, we met again in Paris, purely a stroke o' fate. We had a harmless talk. I ne'r saw her again, 'til we arrived here. That is all there is to it, Hiram."

Hiram was relieved to some extent. "I understand. I was concerned about Albert."

"All has been said and done. Ya need not be worrin', Hiram."

"I appreciate your honesty, Daniel. I will retire, now. I will see you at breakfast."

"Hiram, might I ask, how are ye farin' with me sister?"

Hiram's face broke into a pleased smile and left his friend to his reading.

Abigail enjoyed a luxurious bath in the large tub and retired to the canopy bed. Eloise brought the filled tilting pitcher to sit at her bedside and the heated stone pig, which she placed at Abigail's feet.

"Thank you, Eloise."

"You are welcome, miss. Sleep well."

"You know, Daniel, do you not?"

Incapable of lying, Eloise admitted, "Yes."

"You need not fret over it, Eloise. Daniel is an honorable man and respects your marriage. He would not do anything disapproving. You seem to be nervous around Daniel. Is there a problem?"

"The problem is that I never confided the relationship with my husband. If I were to tell him now, it would be apparent that I kept it a secret all these years. Albert is adamantly opposed to secrets, Miss O'Leardon."

"I think that I may be able to help you... if you help me. A fair exchange of sorts."

"You, help me?"

"I know a way to guarantee that your relationship with your husband will be secure."

"What can you possibly do?"

"Trust me. I assure you that I honor your marriage and I do not intend to return to London with or without a brother who has suffered from the wrath of a jealous husband. But I cannot inform you in advance; it would spoil the plan."

"I am not sure about this proposal, Miss O'Leardon. What is it that you want from me in return?"

"Information...and your promise that you will never tell a living soul that I made this inquiry."

"Information about what?" Eloise looked skeptically and unfolded the quilt at the end of the bed.

"Your master's past."

"I am not certain that he would approve."

"How will he ever find out?"

"What exactly do you want to know?" Eloise spread the quilt across the bed.

"Come closer, I do not want anyone to hear."

Eloise sat down on the chair next to the bed.

"Who have been the women in his life?"

"Very few, that I am aware of. Why do you want to know?"

Abigail answered without hesitation, "The usual reasons. Tell me, Eloise."

"I guess there would be no harm in it. Very well. Naomi was his first love."

"Yes..." Abigail sat up straight.

"But that was decades ago. She has since married his uncle Edward. They fell in love and will soon renew their vows, provided he stays off the ladders."

"Who was next?"

"I have no idea; he was gone for about seventeen years."

"Oh," Abigail slid down disappointed. "Anyone else?"

"I really feel uncomfortable about this conversation, Miss O'Leardon?"

"Eloise, it is all common knowledge. Why should you?"

"I suppose. He spent a few months in London with Allison, Naomi's daughter. Then after a misunderstanding, went off to London alone."

"Naomi's daughter?"

"It was very innocent, Miss O'Leardon. They were friends. Then he met Miss Clayton in London. She will probably be returning for another visit before long."

"Not likely," Abigail said with authority.

"No?" Eloise said disappointedly. "She was a lovely woman."

"Not lovely enough."

"She was the last, as far as I know." Eloise gathered the soiled towels. "He is the charmer, but he does not have the charisma that his uncle has.

Of course, there is none more handsome than Master Hiram. I believe, too, that his quiet mysterious side tends to draw women to him."

"Quiet and mysterious? I find that difficult to imagine." *He can take his haughty, mysterious charm and use it elsewhere.*

"He does appear to be more animated since you arrived. The master has had his moments. I cleaned up the parlor after his rage over Naomi." Eloise's hand quickly covered her mouth, realizing that she had already shared more than enough "information."

"Hiram McDonnally loses his temper?" *Naomi warned me.*

Eloise refrained from responding.

Abigail jerked the covers up to her chin, "I am wise to men and their schemes. They are not to be trusted, Eloise."

"You are young Miss O'Leardon. You cannot possibly believe this is true of all men. What about your brother?" Eloise questioned.

"He is the exception. Thank you, Eloise. You have been very helpful. Tomorrow your troubles will disappear with the March winds. It is a pact, Eloise. You are sworn to secrecy."

Discovering the subversive techniques which Miss O'Leardon, employed, Eloise left the room, unsure of her involvement with the guest. She shivered with the thought of Abigail's last word.

Abigail scooted down beneath the covers. *Duff, why could you have not stayed and shared oats with Homer? Even the McDonnally animals are insufferable!*

Chapter XII

"The Birthday"

"Thou art my life, my love, my heart
The very eyes of me.
And hast command of every part,
To live and die for thee."

—Robert Herrick

Thursday morning, with Sophia's request and Hiram's approval, Albert drove Sophia and Abigail into the village for the day. Daniel enjoyed the McDonnally's extensive library while Hiram made a visit to Brachney Hall, having received word that Edward and Naomi wished to speak with him. Hiram walked to his uncle's home where Naomi greeted him.

"Welcome, Hiram." Naomi turned toward the drawing room. "Edward, Hiram has arrived!" She led Hiram to his uncle where he sat in his wheelchair. "I will leave you two alone for awhile." She continued on to the library.

"Edward! I should have known that nothing could keep you down. Here," he handed Edward the little package, "something to entertain you while you recover. I thought that you would enjoy a little journey *out west* with Zane Grey." Hiram took a chair next to Edward.

"Hiram, this is not necessary," Edward said with sincerity, inquisitively untied the string and then unfolded the paper. "Capital! Riders of the Purple Sage! Thank you, Hiram! Perfect. You may read it, of course, when I am finished." Edward flipped through the pages.

"Frankly, Edward, I have been living in the *wild west*, ever since I met Daniel's sister. She is high-strung and unpredictable, to say the least."

Edward looked up with a grin, "Hiram? I am astounded. There is actually a woman who does not find you to be irresistible?" he teased.

"Perhaps, since you are the expert on outlaws and snakebites, you could instruct me in dealing with Miss O'Leardon," Hiram said in jest.

Naomi returned near the end of the fascinating conversation. Hiram stood with her entry.

"Hiram, confess that you are exaggerating. I met Abigail. She appears a little self-sufficient, but is well-bred and likeable."

"Which reminds me, my apologies for Duff's escape, we were in a hurry to help Harriet with the fire and inadvertently left the gate open," Hiram explained.

Naomi placed her hands on her hips, "Hiram McDonnally, you are covering for her. Either you are quite the gentleman, or your feelings for Miss O'Leardon are not as unfavorable as you have led us to believe," Naomi teased.

"No further discussion of Miss O'Leardon, please. Now, Edward, I have yet to hear your reason for being on the ladder." Hiram quickly diverted the course of the conversation.

"No further discussion of ladders, either. Please sit down, Hiram," Edward insisted.

"Very well, may I ask as to why I was invited here this morning?... Other than to visit with two of my favorite people." Hiram took a chair next to Edward. The serious expressions that befell their faces suggested that ill tidings were in order.

"What has happened?" Hiram leaned toward them.

Naomi handed him the photograph of Vila and the infant Natalia. "Hiram look at this photograph, please."

Hiram took it, examined it and replied, "I am not familiar with either of these people. Should I be?" He flipped it over and read the inscription to Nathan, Naomi's father. "Is this you with your mother, Naomi?"

"No, Hiram, the woman is Vila Ramsey," Edward confirmed.

"Vila? I was too young to remember her. We

knew that they had conspired, but who is this child? This is not my sister, Hannah." Hiram looked curiously at the picture.

"My half sister, Natalia. Vila was her mother." Naomi sat down next to Hiram.

"When was this taken?" Hiram looked closer, for a date.

"This was taken just before Natalia passed on, before Vila kidnapped Hannah," Naomi pointed out.

Hiram sat for a minute pondering the set of circumstances. "She lost her child, your sister, before she kidnapped my sister."

"Yes, Hiram," Naomi concurred.

"So are you suggesting that Vila's loss, her grief over Natalia, may have instigated the kidnapping of my twin?" Hiram stared at the infant in the photograph.

"We both agree that considering the time frame, it is more than likely. It was not only Vila, who grieved. My father has been visiting Natalia's grave for nearly thirty-five years. Difficult to imagine, Nathan displaying affection," Naomi spoke solemnly.

Hiram sat silent. He blamed Nathan and Vila for his sister's lifestyle and for his personal loss of his twin. Hiram believed that Hannah would never feel comfortable being a McDonnally and probably would never return to become an active member of the clan, due to the manner in which she was raised. This had been truly unforgivable in his mind. He had equally held them responsible for his mother's misery, her inability to cope with her loss. On the other hand, Hiram's charitable side could not dismiss the motives of the grief-stricken kidnappers.

Hiram returned shortly to McDonnally Manor and spent the rest of the afternoon with Daniel. Later, Sophia and Abigail arrived. Abigail was talking a mile a minute about the wonderful time that they shared in the village. She described the variety of imported items that she discovered in the mercantile, followed by her impression with the colorful residents of the village.

"Daniel, Dagmar, the Swede at the mercantile, is fascinating and Jon Wiggins, the butcher," she started to laugh, "is incorrigible, with those absurd stories! Then there was Mr. Kilvert, the postman. Sweet man— he and his wife are preparing their cottage for their son, Jake, when he marries. And there was Ian, the most incredibly attractive man on Earth! Do you not agree, Sophia?"

Sophia looked at the expression on her uncle's face that had instantly changed from amusement in listening to Abigail's accounts, to total shock and disapproval.

"He is very—" Sophia was cut-off with her uncle's stern demand.

"Stay away from MacGill! Both of you!" He left his chair and walked over to the window, boiling with anger.

"I beg your pardon! I will see or speak with whomever I please!" Abigail shouted back.

Hiram swung around. "Not with MacGill! Not as long as you are a guest in my house! I am warning you. Do not wander into uncharted waters, or you will regret it. Excuse me; I will have Eloise prepare tea." Hiram left irritated, thinking; she vexes me to the point of near insanity!

Abigail and Sophia spoke not another word about the unsavory, Ian MacGill. When Hiram returned, neither of the women spoke to him. He looked to them suspiciously.

Eloise arrived with the tea. At that moment, Albert burst into the room, nearly scaring the daylights out of all in attendance. He took the tray from his wife and sat it on the table. "Ellie, please sit here." Albert led his wife to the large over-stuffed chair. "Wait here." Abigail smiled confidently with apparent satisfaction. Hiram made note of her irregular reaction, which was quite the opposite of his niece's.

Albert went to the hall and returned carrying a large carton wrapped within a piece of exquisite damask, tied with a red satin ribbon. Albert placed the package on his wife's lap. She stared in awe at the impressive offering before her. Albert then knelt before Eloise with little regard for the audience, particularly Daniel. He looked deep into her heart and soul and recited the following in German:

> "*The minute I heard*
> *My first love story*
> *I started looking for you,*
> *Not knowing how blind that was.*
> *Lovers don't finally meet somewhere.*
> *They're in each other all along.*

Best wishes for your birthday, my dear Ellie."

For Eloise, it was all too beautiful and wonderfully romantic. She reached for Albert's broad shoulders, buried her face in his chest, and wept. After a few minutes of consolation, Eloise opened the gift, a set of hand-painted dishes.

"Guillaume will give you his gift later." Albert reported. Eloise cried again and all in the room experienced some discomfort with the personal expression of love between the man and wife of so many years. All except Daniel, who felt very secure that *his* Ellie was unquestionably with the perfect husband.

A couple hours later, a series of short conversations between the residents of the estate shed light on the unscheduled birthday celebration. Hiram met with Albert to discuss the plans for the upcoming week. As the conversation came to a close, Hiram commented, "Your tribute to your wife was quite moving."

"Thanks to Miss O'Leardon. I nearly forgot."

"Pardon me, Albert, what did you say?"

"Just rambling, sir. I should finish my chores." Albert, embarrassed that he had nearly confessed to forgetting his wife's birthday, left hastily to the cottage.

Later that evening, Eloise took Abigail aside in the upstairs hallway. "What have you done Miss O'Leardon?"

"I simply weighed the odds that your husband did not remember the date of your birthday."

"And?"

"And I asked him if he remembered if today was your birthday."

"Miss O'Leardon, that is unconscionable, it is not my birthday!"

"Eloise, I did nothing wrong, I merely asked him if he remembered *if* today was your birthday. I never said that today was your birthday. I kept my end of the bargain; all is well with the Zigmanns."

Eloise closed her eyes and shook her head.

"Cheer up, Ellie, it is your birthday!"

Abigail smiled and patted Eloise on the back, then went to find Heidi. She found the dog in the kitchen alone in its basket by the stove and walked in cautiously, surprised to find that Heidi made no response to her entry. Unbeknownst to Abigail, Hiram stood silent in the hall watching.

"Hello, little dog, my name is Abigail. It is very important that we become friends." The little dachshund raised its head and listened. "Now if you just stay in that basket, we will both be fine. I am here only to become better acquainted." Heidi wagged her tail, jumped out and ran towards her. Abigail leaped up on a chair. Hiram could barely contain his laughter.

"What are you doing? You were supposed to stay in your basket. Now stay back! Do not come any closer." Heidi ran over to her, stopped and sat up on her haunches, waving her paws. "Oh, what are you doing now? What do you want?" Abigail squatted down closer, still maintaining her position on the chair. "That looks awfully cute. What do you want?"

Hiram entered the room, startling Abigail, who reverted to a standing position on the chair at the sight of him. Hiram walked over to her and for the very first time, he was looking up to her. He explained tenderly, "She wants you to pick her up."

"I knew that," she nervously brushed at her clothes. "I did not want to soil my clothing," Abigail insisted.

Hiram reached down and gently picked up the pup, still waiting patiently. With a very endearing smile, he handed Heidi to Abigail. Hiram's trusting eyes led Abigail to extend her arms and accept the canine companion. She held it without smile or comment for less than a minute, and then returned it to him. Hiram placed Heidi on the floor and offered Abigail a hand. She accepted it, stepped down from the chair and glanced one more time at the dog, which had returned to the basket. She started to leave the kitchen when Hiram's unexpected words detained her.

"Today is not Mrs. Zigmann's birthday. Her birthday is in July. I have it in the employment records." Abigail did not face her accuser, and then left the kitchen to retire. Hiram watched her leave, perplexed by this strange woman who had come into his life.

Hiram left the kitchen to visit his mother's room on the third floor. There he turned the silver key with the green tassel gaining entry to her private room. He took a seat in the chair facing his mother's portrait. His thoughts went immediately to his sister, Hannah, in seeing the resemblance shared with mother and daughter.

"Mother, I found her, your baby Hannah. Tried as I may, Hannah refused to return to the clan and Lochmoor...she should be the one speaking to you now, not I. If Vila had only chosen to take me instead, you might have been alive today. I will try not to disappoint you anymore than I already have... I guess you know that her daughter Sophia is with us. She is God's blessing to us. You would have adored her..." Hiram stood and began his usual pacing.

"A turn of events, Naomi's father is equally responsible for Hannah's kidnapping. He assisted Vila. But as much as I want to hate him, I cannot. The infant Natalia who shares Heaven with you is Naomi's sister, Vila's daughter. I know that you have forgiven them and I want you to know that I will not seek revenge. They grieve for the loss of their child, too." Hiram turned and faced the portrait. "I am not to judge, as you have taught me. That is what brings me here today." He sat down in the chair and folded his hands.

"I need your guidance. Although Miss O'Leardon, Abigail, is intolerable, ridicules me and disrespects me, I am very drawn to her. No other woman has given me such cause to cut myself off from her or to fight for her affections...She appears to hate your son passionately," he said with frustration. He slouched down in the chair and shook his finger, "You ask, *why*? Believe it or not, I truly believe that she may have feelings for me, positive feelings. But she may be fearful to the point of denial. I would not give her the time of day, except that she comes from good stock. Her brother Daniel is a great chap." He sat up.

No, I cannot fool you, dear Mother. I believe that I may love her. "Yes, I loved Naomi. I still do, in a brotherly way. It is different with Abigail. I cannot describe my feelings." Hiram stood and strode across the room several times and then returned to face the portrait.

"It is though everyone is talking about an incredible book that will change your life. Everyday there is someone talking about it. Everywhere you go, everyone you meet treasures this book, but no one will tell you where to find it. You look everywhere, try everything and still fail. You want that book so desperately, that you think about it day and night. And then, you think that you have found it and you open the cover with relief, only to find its contents missing. The search continues."

What do you and our dear Father in Heaven advise? If it is your will, how may I rescue her from her fears and me from this longing to be accepted?

Chapter XIII

"*Civility*"

"Try as I like to find the way'
I never get back by day,
Nor can remember plain and clear
The curious music that I hear."

—Robert Louis Stevenson

Friday morning, breakfast was prepared, hot and delicious for the inhabitants of McDonnally Manor. Abigail and Daniel arrived punctually at eight-thirty as requested the night before. Eloise was a stickler for serving meals promptly at the proper temperature. Hiram found her dedication to be admirable and desirable. However, a nearly sleepless night after the visit with Naomi and Edward resulted in Hiram joining his guests nearly twenty minutes after the designated time. Eloise served the guests and held her tongue, although irritated with the master's tardiness.

Hiram took his seat without a word, just a simple greeting nod.

Insulted by Hiram's tardiness, Abigail mocked, "Daniel, Eloise said breakfast was served at a half past eight, did she not? Perhaps, punctuality is required by the guests alone, not of the infallible *Grand Master*."

Sophia held her spoon in mid-air, cringing and waiting for her uncle to speak, expecting the worst. Hiram's mood did not lend itself well to Abigail's criticism. Having suffered hours of soul searching, he could bear no more. He slammed both fists down on the table, and stood.

"Miss O'Leardon, I want o speak with you in the study!" he demanded.

"Whatever for, Mr. McDonnally? Is it not enough that you were not here to properly greet us, that you must also take pleasure in disturbing my meal?" she replied indignantly.

"Now! Miss O'Leardon."

Abigail jumped with the second outburst, excused herself, and followed quite leisurely to the study. Her brother shook his head disparagingly, knowing that his sister had overstepped her bounds. Hiram pulled the doors to the study closed behind Abigail and disregarding any interest in her comfort, refused to offer her a chair.

Hiram began pacing. "My patience is wearing thin. Frankly, you have driven me to my wit's end...I do not know where to begin."

"Ah! A master of rhyme, as well," Abigail said with a shrewd grin.

Hiram swung around to meet the witty wench. "Woman, your insolence appalls me!"

"And your bringing me here, to bully me, appalls me!" Abigail retorted.

"Aye, bully you? You have made me a source of ridicule and a prisoner of torment in my own home! I will not be the object of your revenge, nor will I be punished for the sins of those before me!"

"If you are not deserving of this fate, why do you tolerate it?" she asked coolly and moved in on him. "I will tell you why. Because you are conceited and arrogant and you believe that I am weak like every other woman. You are convinced that you can win me over with your wealth and your transparent charm until you take a fancy to the next young beauty, as you did with Naomi and Allison!"

"Enough!" Hiram threw up his arms in rage.

"I had thought that Elizabeth had wronged you, but after reconsidering, I respect and honor her decision to end the relationship without an explanation. Because you, *my dear man,* pretend to be the hurt inexperienced school boy, whining to my brother, yet you discard women like yesterday's trash in the dustbin!"

"Never address me again as 'your dear man' as the implications disgust me! Leave this room at once," he pointed to the door, "or I shan't be responsible for neither my words, nor my actions!"

Abigail marched out closing the study doors behind her, satisfied that she said her piece, but jumped when the crashing of a chair on the other side of the door gave her second thoughts.

Hiram stood with his arms raised, his eyes to the heavens and his fists clenched. *Woman, why do I love you! Have I gone completely mad?*

Abigail collected herself, returned to the breakfast table, showing no signs of being rattled by the confrontation and resumed eating her meal.

"Eloise, more coffee, please," Abigail requested when a second crash from the study sent a chill down her spine. Abigail continued to eat, charading her indifference, whereas Daniel and Sophia exhibited notable anxiety. A minute later, Sophia's eyes widened and Daniel's closed with the pounding of the approaching footsteps of the master's boots.

Hiram paused at Daniel's side, "May I please speak with you in the study, Daniel?"

So it is "may, I please" for my brother, Abigail thought with irritation.

"Ay, Hiram." Daniel wiped his mouth and followed Hiram, expecting the worst.

The sight of the rubble in the study left Daniel no choice. He shamefully offered, "We will be leavin' as soon as our bags are packed."

"On the contrary, Daniel, I would like you to stay."

"Stay and send Abigail back to London?"

"No, actually, I would like for you and your sister to extend your visit for a few more weeks."

"Hiram, have ya gone mad? Abby has done this to ya."

"I will contact a friend in London to send someone over to your bookstore to assist Oliver," Hiram added in a calm, controlled voice. "And yes,

Daniel, perhaps I am mad. I have lost one too many battles, blinded by my pride. My eyes are wide open now and I have your sister to thank for that. I told you that I would not walk away, nor would I give up on your sister."

"But, Hiram, ye only have so many rooms in this house to suffer the damage. And Abby is more—"

"I know what Abby is. That is where *I* have the advantage. She does not know what I am; she only thinks that she does. I will not rest, until she does. Please accept my apologies for disrupting your breakfast. And Daniel, I *am* working on keeping my temper in check."

Daniel reviewed the ruins. "Aye, I can see a definite improvement," he raised his brow.

"I said I was *working* on it..." Hiram picked up the now three-legged table and tried to stand it in position. It toppled to the floor. Hiram sighed, "Shall we go?"

Daniel stopped and stared, perplexed, at his strange comrade and his masochistic plan. He stepped over the broken pieces of the chair and small table and entered the hall.

"Keep in mind, Hiram, that you are not the only one that is ill-tempered. Abigail's last suitor ended up wearing a pot o' stew," Daniel warned. Hiram placed his arm around his dear friend and patted his back with a confident smile.

Abigail and Sophia remained neutral and spoke not a word to one another; Eloise watched and waited anticipating an explosion when Hiram and Daniel returned. The two men entered the dining room, peaceably and took their places at the table.

"Eloise, please discard Daniel's and my food and prepare other portions."

"Yes, sir."

The suspense of the conference in the study was taking its toll on the two ladies at the table and Hiram was enjoying every extended minute of it. Eloise returned with the freshly heated food.

Abigail could stand it no longer and tested the water, "What are our plans for today?"

Hiram said nothing, further exasperating his guest. After another couple of minutes, he laid down his fork and addressed her with a confident smile. "I think that we shall take the carriage up to Duncan Ridge. Then later this evening we shall attend the engagement at Brachney Hall. We shall leave at noon. Please prepare a basket for noon tea, Eloise."

"Yes, sir," Eloise looked suspiciously toward Abigail.

This little agenda was not at all what Abigail expected and turned to her brother for confirmation. Daniel's eyes never left his plate. Hiram sipped his tea and then wiped his mouth with his napkin.

"Excuse me, I have an engagement. Miss O'Leardon, Daniel, Sophia."

Hiram returned to the study and wrote a short list of names. He placed it in an envelope, addressed to Edward, and gave it to Albert, instructing its delivery. Hiram then met with Eloise in the kitchen. "Eloise, if you please, there is a bit of cleaning needed in the study. I do apologise. What would I do without you?"

"Yes, sir, I will take care of it as soon as I finish the dishes."

"Thank you." Hiram went directly up to his room and closed the door. He walked over to the mirror and addressed his reflective counterpart.

"If Edward can face the world without you, so shall I."

At twelve noon, Albert sat in the carriage, posted in the drive, waiting for his passengers. Abigail was the first to arrive. Albert greeted her, assisted her into the carriage, and met his wife with the basket at the main door. Albert placed the basket inside the carriage and resumed his position at the reins. Abigail waited nervously, fidgeting with the buttons on her jacket, upset that Daniel had given her no information as to the content of his conversation with Hiram and no clue as to his demeanor after her earlier conflict with his friend. She became more anxious as the minutes passed.

Finally, the door to the house opened and her host appeared. Abigail's eyes widened with his disarming appearance. He had never looked more handsome, his striking clothes were tailored to perfection. However, one element of his image took a greater toll, lessening her resistance more than the others; her jaw dropped at the sight of his clean-shaven face. The removal of his beard took ten years with it. His younger countenance shone like his ebony curls. Hiram climbed into the carriage across from his very uncomfortable guest.

"Good afternoon, Miss O'Leardon, you are looking quite bonnie," Hiram remarked, enjoying the shock in Abigail's expression.

Abigail struggled to speak as she sat in awe. *This is not cricket...I will be strong* she thought skeptically and offered no gratitude for his unexpected compliment. Finally, she found the words, "I cannot imagine what is keeping Daniel."

"I can. He is visiting Edward and Naomi at Brachney Hall." Hiram tapped the window and the carriage moved forward.

"We will be meeting him there?" Abigail demanded.

"Eventually."

Abigail sat back admiring the hillside, relieved that Daniel would soon be joining them. She fought the urge to look at the ever-so-appealing passenger across from her, telling herself that she must never drop her guard and become another chapter in his history.

As they approached the adjoining estate, the carriage never decreased its speed, nor did it stop. Abigail was lost to confusion, "Tell him to stop the carriage for Daniel!" Her words fell on deaf ears.

Hiram settled back unconcerned with his guest's demands.

"Daniel will not approve of this!" she argued.

"He already has," Hiram stated calmly as he enjoyed the passing landscape. "Splendid day."

Violently opposed to her abduction, she made a move for the carriage door, when the master's boot quickly swung up to the seat next to her, blocking the exit. Abigail sat down scowling.

"Miss O'Leardon, you should smile more. It is much more becoming. Sit back and enjoy the most beautiful part of Scotland."

She fixed her gaze out the left window, ignoring her captor and his tempting face.

"You never did explain why you do not share your brother's horrid accent," he laughed.

Abigail turned only long enough to answer, trying desperately to avoid the distraction of Hiram's deep dimples, enhanced by his smile.

"I do not believe in accents."

Hiram folded his hands in his lap and nodded approvingly, thinking, *you are one strange woman. I cannot imagine what you will say or do next.*

Silence prevailed while the coach left the main road and through a series of turns, slowly wound its way up to a spot on top Duncan Ridge. Hiram tapped the window and Albert brought the horse to a halt. Hiram climbed from the carriage with the basket.

Abigail stuck her head out, "Albert, take me home!" Albert remained quiet. Abigail made her first mistake by stepping out of the carriage to reprimand the driver when Hiram signaled Albert to leave.

Abigail chased after him, "Albert! You come back here!"

The carriage sped away. Abigail still raging with anger turned to Hiram to voice her disapproval.

Hiram remained calm. "You shan't worry, Albert will return in a few hours. You are perfectly safe with me. I have but chosen to demonstrate to you that I am not the proud ogre that you have made me out to be." His thoughts continued while he opened the basket. *I will provide you with an afternoon that you will always remember. If your attitude does not improve, your experience at Brachney Hall will be one that you will wish to forget.*

Hiram, ignoring Abigail's ranting and raving, took the cloth from the basket and spread it across the ground. "Now shall we make the best of this glorious day and share a *civil* breaking of bread?" Hiram asked in a very controlled, yet sincere manner.

Abigail snatched the cloth in disgust, rolled, twisted it, and cast it to the ground. She stood steaming before him with her hands now tight on her hips. Hiram looked at the cloth, then the violator. He sat down on the ground, chose a piece of meat from the basket, and unwrapped it as though nothing had happened.

"You apparently have not the remotest idea as to what *civil* implies." He said between bites. "I shall educate you. *Civil* refers to the ability to treat your host with respect, particularly in the case when the host, who would choose to take pride in introducing his guests to members of his community, has offered to share his home, his pantry and his time." *Give me strength.* He chose another piece of meat from the basket, unwrapped it and reached out to offer it to her, giving her yet another chance to make amends.

Abigail kept her hands gripped at her waist and thrust her right foot back and with one swift kick to the ground, sprayed her host with a rain of dust. Hiram, having never tolerated the wrath of such an ill-tempered woman, fought his instincts to retaliate. He sat for a moment, brushing the dust from his clothing. *Keep it in check, keep it in check.* He managed to maintain control and said coolly, "Now, since you choose to act like an animal, I will treat you as one." He tossed the piece of meat at her feet.

Abigail wasted no time in stomping on his offering and grinding it into the dirt. Then Abigail made her second mistake. She turned in a huff and headed down the hill in the direction of his estate.

"Have a pleasant walk, Miss O'Leardon. They may have chased the snakes out of Ireland, but we have our fair share!" he called to her.

Abigail hesitated, and then continued fighting the rough terrain. Hiram watched trying to maintain his temper with her departure. He devoured all the foodstuffs and sat brooding while her form diminished in the distance. He questioned his method, which appeared to have failed miserably. He ran his hand over his smooth face and stood. *Perhaps, she preferred the beard.* He kicked the basket aside and left the ridge to follow her.

Abigail continued, her pace hindered only by the undergrowth.

"How dare he treat me in such a manner, he and his fine clothes and that...that *face*! Daniel will have his hide for this, making me walk this distance!" she grumbled. Her mutterings continued as she held up her hem and marched back toward the manor. Exasperated by the poor footing and necessary endurance required to continue, Abigail plopped down in the waving grass.

"And he thinks he can charm me with those dimples!"

"Aye? Taking a wee rest, Miss O'Leardon?"

Abigail's heart stopped with the familiar voice, turned and looked up.

"Quite a trek back, Miss O'Leardon. It can be a bit tricky if you are not familiar with this part of the country." Hiram shook his head with doubt. "Perchance, you were in need of company to join you? Someone to lead the way?"

"Indeed not, I am merely enjoying the view," she remarked staring up at him as he loomed over her.

"Indeed you are," he cracked a roguish smile.

Her eyes quickly returned to the hillside. *You arrogant beast!*

"Very well, then, good day, my lady. I trust I shall see you at the festivities at Brachney Hall this evening. I would not tarry too long; Naomi and Edward are expecting us to be prompt." He continued down the hillside.

You insufferable...Mr. McDonnally! Embittered, she watched him move into the hills possibly taking with him her only hope of finding her way back to the manor. Her instincts to surrender screamed in her conscience with each of his steps. Despite her fears, her pride overrode any inclination to call out to him. Soon, his figure disappeared into a pine forest. Abigail sat pouting, glancing up intermittently at the foreboding woods in the distance.

Beaten at her own game, she called in desperation, "Hiram! Hiram come back!." However, the music of the winds were such that her voice, like she, was lost in the hills.

Chapter XIV

"Lost and Found"

"The speedy gleams the darkness swallow'd;
Loud, deep, and lang, the thunder bellow'd:
That night, a child might understand
The deil had business on his hand."

—Robert Burns

Hiram paused in the pinewoods and sat down on a fallen log, waiting for the arrival of his disgruntled guest. In the meantime, Abigail stood up and surveyed the hills. *I think the road is more to my liking.* She turned to the right and began her search for the road. The obscuring rolling hills brought new landscape into view. She stopped to rest on a large boulder and swiveled around taking in all aspects of the countryside. Her thoughts drifted back to her irrepressible feelings for the Master of McDonnally Manor. *You are so impossible, yet so...* She made a few more turns on the stone and rose to continue to the road. Without any notice to her orientation, she continued off in the opposite direction as the sky darkened with the ominous black of incoming clouds. She saw a cluster of pines over the next hill. *The trees, yes the woods that he entered. Or are they? McDonnally Manor must be on the other side.* She pushed on through to the clearing and entered yet another forest of thick pines, watching for a break to the fields. *How do I get out of here?* She changed directions several times in an attempt to find her way out. Instead, she found herself traveling in circles. Her legs could carry her no longer, so she sat down on a bed of pine needles and leaned against a tree trunk. She stretched out her legs, aching from her journey. Hungry and exhausted she now found herself surrounded with near darkness.

Her fears took hold. Clenching her hands in her lap, she began to pray. "Dear Father, please send me assistance. I am sorry I acted without thought to the consequences, but it is getting late and I am so tired." She tried to position herself more comfortably. "Hiram, where are you? And you call yourself a good host, Master McDonnally, leaving your guest starving and cold without even a map. You make me so angry! And Daniel, my own brother! She closed her eyes, "If I only had a piece of that chicken." Shortly she fell to sleep, hungry and exhausted.

Hiram had returned to the edge of the wood to look for Abigail. Seeing no trace of the obstinate woman, he started combing the hills frantically without any success. With each new hill, he called out to her, without response. He moved quickly back to the area where Albert had stopped the carriage and looked to every direction. He realized that he had covered every possible hill between there and the woods and immediately headed west toward the road. He sprinted through the meadows calling her name. *She probably made her way back to the road. Someone has given her a ride back* he rationalized.

Within a half hour, he was on the road heading back to the estate, distraught with worry. *Where are you, Abigail?* He watched both sides of the road until Brachney Hall came into view. He darted toward the window of his uncle's mansion where Naomi and Edward were entertaining Daniel. Hiram stood hidden in the shadows like a small child who had lost an expensive heirloom. With no evidence of Abigail's presence, he rushed onward to his home and entered the main door. He went up to the second floor to Abigail's room, and knocked on the door. No response. He pounded harder. Nothing. He opened the door, went in, and scanned the room for anything to show that she had been there. He shot down the hall to Sophia's bedroom; the door was ajar and the room was vacant. A strong sense of doom fell over him, leading him to the window. Hiram stood motionless watching the mammoth storm brewing. "Abigail," he panicked.

Thunder boomed in the distance. Hiram ran full speed down the stairs, glanced into the empty parlor, and ran into the kitchen where he found Eloise icing a cake to take to Brachney Hall. Out of breath he inquired, "Eloise, have you seen Miss O'Leardon?"

"Your beard, sir..."

"Yes, now, please, have you seen her?"

"No, sir, not since noon. I thought that she was with you."

Hiram grabbed Eloise's shoulders. "Is she with Sophia?"

"No, sir. I just spoke with Sophia in the study," Eloise reported fearfully.

He relinquished his grip. "Sorry. Eloise." His tormented eyes darted hastily to the window framing the darkening sky. "Eloise, not a word of this conversation!"

"No, sir." Hiram sped to the hall pulling on his cap and overcoat as he headed toward the backdoor. "Where are you going, sir?"

"To get a horse!" Hiram fled out the door.

Eloise called after him, "Be careful, sir!"

Hiram ran to the back gate and unlatched it. His boots pounded through the muddy fields leading to Edward's barn where he pulled open the doors and snatched a bridle from the wall. He opened the stall door to the restless white Hannoverian. "Easy lad, easy." He slipped the bit in its mouth, pulled the bridle up over its ears, and tightened the strap. He led the horse out of the stall and saddled it up. In one swift movement, he mounted. The horse swung up its head as its hooves dug in, blasting out into the pasture to the north side of the estate. Hiram signaled the horse to a halt and dismounted to open the gate. The wind whirled around him as he climbed back into the saddle and snapped the rein ends, urging the steed onward. Hiram stood in the stirrups, leaned forward as the horse stretched out his neck, and lunged forward, pulling into the bit. Hiram's coattails flapped behind him as the horse went into a full gallop. Its ears were pinned back, chest heaving and nostrils flaring as it moved, across the cobblestones. Its stride never broke until the road split and converged to the right into the narrow dirt path. Hiram's eyes were fastened to the road, watching for any sign of life.

In the meantime, Abigail awoke to the eerie wind whistling across the mist-laden moors; the darkness was closing in around her. A friendly male voice behind her, startled her.

"Lassie, ye wouldna be lost would ye?"

"Hiram?" She turned and looked up to a large man dressed in dark clothing and leading a horse. Her eyes were slowly adjusting to the darkness. She tried to focus on the man's face. It was not Hiram. Abigail stood and straightened her skirt, nervously anticipating the stranger's next move. She dare not admit that she was in fact, hopelessly lost.

In the distance, Hiram's horse was now gliding steadily down the path like a white specter. He pulled the reins to the right, directing the horse up into the hills. Descending on the spot where he last saw Abigail, horse and rider moved as one. Random lightning strikes lit up the sky. Hiram's heart pounded, increasingly fearful for Abigail's safety. *What if I cannot find her? Where is she? Something is wrong. I can feel it.* "Abigail! Abigail!"

Hiram knew the foothills like the rooms of the mansion, but the darkness was hampering. He cantered up the next hill to look for the crest of the ridge, trying to get his bearings. There was nothing familiar, no landmarks. Hiram began to panic and the horse sensed it. He traversed the hills in every direction, circling back and forth calling, "Abigail, answer me!" Thunder crashed in the distance and the horse reared, but Hiram kept his seat and sank into the saddle. "Easy, Duff" After a couple more turns, he rode east to the pine forest near the ridge.

In the forest, the stranger moved close to Abigail. Her blood ran cold; petrified of the stranger's possible intentions.

"Might I take ye home?" he offered in a sinister tone, reached out, and grasped her shoulder. Abigail's heart pounded with terror. Panic stricken, she pulled away only to find her arm bound by his grasp. "Aye, Lassie, I *will* take ye home." She started to scream when his other hand clamped over her mouth. Abigail began to struggle, pulling with all her strength to escape.

At the edge of the forest, Hiram quickly dismounted and entered the woods. He led the horse cautiously, shouting in desperation, "Abigail, Abigail, where are you?" The scoundrel immediately set her free, "Later, Lassie," he warned. He mounted his horse and set off rapidly through the trees. Abigail dropped to the ground sobbing.

Drawn by the sound of her whimpering, Hiram ran toward the small huddled form several yards away. He drew nearer to the figure, "Abigail?" he shouted. "Abby!" He dropped down beside her, pulled his coat off, and wrapped it around her. He gently lifted her chin. "Oh, Abby," he said compassionately and held her close, observing her unknown fragility. Tears streamed down her cheeks, which she fought to wipe away with the hem of her sleeve.

Her voice trembled, "Hiram?"

"Aye, Abby, I have come for you. Are you all right?" He moved closer, wrapping his arms around her. He placed his head next to hers. "What are you doing here?"

"I was lost. I thought you were not going to come," she broke down and wept in his arms. He tightened the coat around her, rocking her gently, regretting every minute of the past day.

"Come along. We are going home." He placed an arm around her waist to help her stand.

"No, Hiram! I am afraid," she whispered as she glanced around nervously.

"Abigail, you need not be afraid of me," he said, carefully sliding her hair away from her face.

"No...there was a man, he— I tried to find the road, and then I was so tired and I awoke and he was here beside me— this horrid man," Abigail whimpered.

"Did he harm you?" Hiram demanded, as gently as possible, now inflamed with outrage.

"No, he fled when he heard your calling." Her tears trickled to his hands, which lovingly cradled her face. Hiram looked beyond into the darkness, then back to Abigail. "Abby," he said sympathetically. He shook his head. *Dear God, forgive me.*

She buried her face in his chest, shivering and mumbling, "I am sorry. I am behaving like an infant."

"You are safe now. We are going home, love." He scooped her up and lifted her into the saddle. He led the horse back out into the meadow, mounted behind Abigail and signaled the horse back toward the road. Hiram held the reins with Abigail snuggled close within his extended arms. They hastened forward. Before long, they heard the welcomed cobblestones beneath the hooves, which denoted the completion of half the journey with only a couple remaining miles.

In the distance, Hiram saw a glimmer of lights and heard the clacking of hooves. Within a few minutes, Hiram was lifting Abigail into the coach. "Albert, take us home and be quick about it," Hiram instructed. He unlatched the bridle from Edward's horse and pulled it from its head. Then with a swat with the reins, he commanded, "Go home lad!" The horse galloped off to the familiar barn. Hiram climbed in beside Abigail and gently pulled her under his arm. Eloise was sitting across from them, sick with worry. She quickly took the woolen blanket from her lap, unfolded it and tucked it around Abigail. Eloise took a jar of hot broth from her bag, removed the lid and handed it to Hiram.

"Please, take a drink and give her some," Eloise instructed.

"Thank you, Eloise, for everything." He nudged Abigail and brought the jar to her lips. "Drink, love." Abigail awoke slowly with the warming steam from the jar; the pleasant aroma enticed her to drink. She sipped it slowly, barely capable of keeping her eyes open.

"Albert saw you running to the barn. I had to tell him."

"As you should have," Hiram confirmed. "You obviously, have not spoken to Daniel."

"No, sir." Eloise looked on, sympathetically.

"Just as well. It is my responsibility." Hiram then pulled the blanket close up around Abigail. He stared straight ahead, stern and silent, enraged with himself and the unknown offender. Before long they were back safely at the manor. Hiram never carried a more precious load, feeling no self-pity for the task ahead. Although her weight grew heavy in his arms, moving slowly up the stairs, the weight on his heart with the regret for having left her in the field that afternoon was heavier by far.

"Thank you, sir," Abigail looked up at him as they entered the bedroom.

He could not bear to make eye contact, "I am not deserving of your gratitude. My ignorance and negligence have done this to you. You are tired, hungry, chilled to the bone and were terrorized because of my arrogance. I should be horse-whipped, or worse." He sat her on the bed and went to his room to make a change of clothes while Eloise prepared the weary guest for bed. Hiram lifted the hairbrush from the bureau and looked in the mirror above it. His contempt for the man in the glass forced him to slam it down, fiercely. He walked over to the window. The sky was remarkably clearer. He looked to the heavens. *I have failed you, Mother, again. I have not acted in the manner of a respectable member of the McDonnally clan.* He lifted his jacket from the tree stand, left the room and knocked on Abigail's door. Eloise opened it and invited him in.

"She had some toast and tea, Master. Her brother just left. He wants to speak with you in the parlor, sir."

"Thank you, Eloise. I would like a moment with Miss O'Leardon." Eloise left them and Hiram walked over to the bed where Abigail was apparently sleeping peacefully. "What have I done to you?" He closed his eyes.

"You saved me," a sweet voice replied.

Hiram looked to the pale angelic face below him, pulled the chair up next to the bed, and sat down. "Abigail, understand that I never saved you. I punished you in the worst way. I took you to Duncan Ridge against your will and then abandoned you. You have despised me from the beginning and now I have given you justification for your animosity." His jet-black eyes softened with compassion. "Did you recognize the man?"

"It was dark and I could not see his face very well. Please let it go, I was not harmed. This is not necessary."

"What was his height, his age? What horse did he ride? I need to know." Hiram left the chair, breathing hard, trying to suppress his anger.

Abigail complied, observing his distress. "He was tall and large framed. An older man, a Scot. It was dark, but I believe that his horse was black or bay without markings on its face. I am not certain."

"I am not familiar with anyone of that description, in this part of the country." He walked over to the window, "I will try to make the remainder of your stay as comfortable as possible, and then you may return to London and find someone worthy of your attention." He turned to face her, "I only hope that someday you will be capable of erasing this entire event from your memory. I have dishonored you, my dearest friend, my clan and myself... now I have to speak with your brother. Again, my humblest apologies, Good night Miss O'Leardon." Hiram started to leave.

"May I speak with you for a minute more, sir?"

"It can wait. You need to sleep."

Chapter XV

"Children and Advice"

"I hold it true, whate'er befall;
I feel it, when I sorrow most;
'Tis better to have loved and lost
Than never to have loved at all."

—Alfred Lord Tennyson

Hiram left Abigail for the evening and met Daniel in the parlor. Daniel added more peat to the fire and invited Hiram to sit with him. A natural "pacer" Hiram found the confinement of a chair uncomfortable, but felt the sincerity of his apology and confession required full eye contact. He pulled up a chair across from Daniel.

"Daniel, I do not know how to express my grieved apologies for this incident, although they are of little value in repairing the damage that I have done. I acted without thought or regard to anyone other than myself, resulting in your sister suffering the consequences. You love your sister, Daniel. You are her protector and she is your foremost concern. I have betrayed both of you, unforgivably. I understand if you wish to terminate our relationship without reservation."

Daniel's concerned eyes stared into Hiram's, dark with regret. "Hiram, I have always thought o' ya as a younger brother, even though I am nearly old enough to be ya father. I heard ev'ry word that ya said. But I, too, spoke wi' Abby. She believes that ya were bein' the good host and she left wit' out good cause." Hiram shook his head, but Daniel continued. "Abby should hae stayed wi' ya, despite her temper." Hiram could stand it no longer, he left his chair and began to pace.

"No matter, I should have never left her alone in the hills. She told you about the scoundrel in the woods?"

"Hiram, she came to no harm and she *has* learned an important lesson. Abigail is a pig-headed, woman. I shan't hold you responsible for her actions. But, I have one request o' ya."

Hiram stopped, "What, Daniel? Anything. I will find this man and he will be brought to justice."

"The man was probably just passin' through. Abby said his horse was laden with bedrolls and saddlebags. All I ask is that ya speak wi' Abby. Listen to her. I think her attitude is changin'. Ya promised me that ya wouldna walk away."

Hiram sat down and rested his head in his hands, "Daniel I can grant any wish, but that. Your sister has suffered enough. I will not complicate her life any further with my horrific misconduct. I assured her, as I do you, that I will try to make your stay as pleasant as possible." He walked to the mantle.

"Who would ye be protectin'? Abigail or yerself?"

Hiram's brows knitted slightly. Daniel walked over to his dear friend and placed his hand on his shoulder.

"Hiram, a bit o' advice from an ol' man...dunna quit the race 'fore 'tis finished. 'Tis over when the heart is lost to another. Yer new face, Hiram, is deservin' o' a new beginnin'."

Daniel left Hiram to mull over his words, walked to the end of the hall and entered the kitchen. He looked around the room remembering his discussion with Eloise and his promise to her. He went over to the window and found the lights burning brightly in the caretaker's cottage and stood there for a brief period.

"Perhaps, we should be headin' home, Abby."

Daniel left the kitchen and went directly to the study, dimly lit by an oil lamp. He adjusted the lamp to enhance the visibility of the countless volumes. He chose a small book of poetry and opened it carefully on the table. He removed his wallet and pulled the ribbon free. He bookmarked the page with it and closed the book reverently. He held it tightly with both hands like the last lifeline on a sinking ship. He focused on the cover, then lessened his grip, took a deep breath and replaced the volume to the bookshelf. He blew out the lamp and returned to his room for the remainder of the evening.

Hiram sat in the parlor facing the blazing fire, battling his better judgment and his undeniable desire to take Daniel's advice. *How can I let her go?*

"Uncle, Hiram?"

Hiram turned to his niece, "Come in, Sophia."

"Uncle Hiram! Your face! You look so...so young."

Hiram tightened his lips and looked uncomfortably away from his niece's examination.

"You did this for her, did you not?" Sophia asked pleased with the change.

"You would be prudent in not making assumptions, young lady."

"Naomi, made a short visit with Abigail," Sophia reported and took a place in the chair adjacent to him.

"Naomi is a good woman. I need to apologize to her, and Edward as well, for disrupting their evening. It was very generous of them to honor Daniel and his sister with a special gathering. I am responsible for spoiling it."

"Uncle...women do queer things at times, without thinking," she looked at the ring still stuck on her finger."

"Men do, as well. I abandoned Daniel's sister in the moors this afternoon."

"Uncle, Abigail confessed that she had the opportunity to go with you, but neglected to take it."

"Sophia, I am not offering excuses, but Miss O'Leardon has made me so incredibly vexed that I cannot think clearly when I am in her presence or elsewhere. I left her without thinking or caring about the danger to which I subjected her. My behavior was deplorable and unacceptable. No man should allow the likes of any woman to distract him to the point that he neglects his duties as a protector, Sophia." Hiram got up and began pacing. "A man needs to have his wits about him," he added sternly.

"I do not mean to be impertinent, but in observation, I find it very interesting that a man lacking such wits, shaved off his beard and had the ingenuity to invite a roomful of available women to his uncle's home. Especially, with the intention of provoking jealousy in a certain beautiful adversary."

Hiram looked at his niece with confusion.

"With such short notice, Uncle Edward summoned me to do your bidding." Sophia attempted to lighten the atmosphere.

"Miss McDonnally, might I remind you, as to whom you are addressing," he rebuked, returning his gaze to the fire, embarrassed with his schoolboy tactics. "Sophia, my attempts have been in vain and I am ashamed of my conduct. I have not only been at war with *her*, since the first day we met, but with myself. I have tried to maintain the front, but I am not a soldier like my forefathers. I am not prepared to fight any longer. I tried to mix water with oil and the results were disastrous."

"Retreating, again? I am surprised, Uncle. In the short time that I have known you, I honestly can say that I did not expect this of you. In viewing your confrontations with Abigail, I assure you that there was a mutual passion for the conflict. Throughout history, it has been quite common for couples to share animosity before their relationship develops in to one of a congenial, lasting relationship." Sophia spoke with authority and encouragement.

"You, my dear lassie, are inexperienced and a hopeless romantic."

"Look at the facts. We have a case right here in Lochmoor. Allison and Guillaume fought like a cat and dog and look at them now, in love for all eternity."

Hiram shook his head.

"Uncle, do you need more evidence to support my theory?"

"Now you sound like your aunt, Naomi."

"Uncle, there is a beautiful woman upstairs who has struggled brutally to keep her eyes off of you. I cannot imagine how she suffered when she saw your face."

Hiram moved in his chair, uneasy with Sophia's speculation.

"Naturally her only defense against your incredible charm was to insult you," Sophia's enthusiasm increased.

"*Naturally*," Hiram rolled his eyes upward.

"Do you realize that in your absence, that poor woman dragged herself through the streets on an intense mission to learn as much about you as possible?"

"Dragged herself?" Hiram smiled with amusement.

"You laugh, but it can be described as nothing less than pathetic! Her interest in you verges on being seriously obsessive! Do you want an example? I have several dozen."

"I am not in the mood for creative exaggeration. This is not necessary, Sophia."

"I think that it is. You cannot act properly without all the sordid facts strewn before you. When Abigail and I were in the village, we entered the butcher shop to meet Jon Wiggins. His nephew was there playing on the floor. Do you know what her first remark was?"

"Something to the effect that I am as distasteful as Wiggins' tales?"

"No, not at all. She said, and I quote, 'Do you think that Hiram looked like him, as a lad?' Mr. Wiggins' nephew of course had a head full of black curls and your coloring."

"A natural observation."

"Do you need more? Another example: When we met Mr. Kilvert making his delivery on horseback, not but ten minutes later, she inquired as to whether or not *you* were a good horseman."

"A common inquiry, Sophia."

"Very well, I was not going to resort to divulging this information, for fear that it would go to your head, and expose Abigail, but I have no other choice. Now, please, hold your temper. When Abigail saw Ian MacGill strutting around the square, during his usual morning routine, in *actuality*, she whispered to me that Ian was not half the man you are." Hiram's brows knitted with the mere mention of Ian.

"She said that not only that you were over twice his stature, but more handsome by tenfold! Now, what do you think, Uncle?"

Hiram dropped his head, surprised by the compliment, which further complicated his decision.

"Well, Uncle, will you not save this woman from her devouring infatuation?"

Hiram raised his head and spoke ominously, "More than likely, I already have. Your accounts have no significance at this point; they occurred prior to my revolting behavior today. Any lingering positive feelings that Miss O'Leardon has for me are only temporary and inspired by her misguided gratitude for finding her. Tomorrow, Sophia, this clever woman will realize that I am not *half* the man that she thought I was."

The next morning, Naomi left Allison chatting with Abigail at McDonnally Manor. The two women got along famously, however avoided any discussion of their common link, Hiram. Naomi, after recovering from the shock of Hiram's reminiscent youthful face, conversed with him briefly and returned to Brachney Hall to take breakfast to Edward, who had not found a suitable cook for hire.

Naomi found Edward examining his reclining chair, "*My Royal Chair,* will come in handy, Naomi. It has sat idle for nearly ten years. I bought it when they were first marketed. Yes, I had visions of coming home from business trips, stretching out in it and relaxing until I fell asleep. I never seemed to find the time."

"Well, I am thankful that you purchased it. Remember what Dr. Kelly said about keeping that leg elevated for a good portion of the day," Naomi reminded.

"Yes, *nurse*," Edward agreed. "How is Guillaume doing? I have not seen him in a couple of weeks."

"Edward McDonnally, he just moved back to the cottage a few days ago. Sometimes I think that you were the one with the head injury. You should be content to know that Guillaume has improved enough to return home."

"I suppose, but it is lonely here, now."

"You did not appear to be too lonely with all those women fawning over you last night. As for your loneliness, I have a cure. I have invited Hiram and his guests over on Sunday for a few hands of pinochle. I spoke with Hiram, this morning. He sends his sincere apologies for last night."

"Yes, it is a shame that he left me to entertain all those lonely lassies," he peeked rascally at Naomi, who ignored his comment. "How *is* the illusive, Miss O'Leardon?"

"Eloise said that she had a good night's sleep. I think Hiram is suffering more than she is. Eloise says that he feels remorsefully responsible for the incident."

"I can certainly empathize with him," he looked regretfully at Naomi's scarred face.

"Now, Edward, let the past go," Naomi said lovingly, placing the aromatic meal before him.

"Smells, delicious." He lifted his fork, "Hiram seems to travel through life, hand-in-hand with misfortune. I guess that is true of all the McDonnally's, I included."

"Edward, we are going to put an end to all that, correct?" Naomi sat down next to him.

"Most definitely. You take such good care of me. Although, Hiram will not be sharing good memories of Duncan Ridge with Abigail, as we do. I am very curious to meet Miss O'Leardon, but I have one question."

"What is that, Edward?"

"How am I going to play cards?"

Naomi smiled, "This is how." Naomi went to the corner cupboard and brought out a slotted board about a foot long. "Angus made it for you. You see, you place the cards upright in the slots."

"Capital. Be sure to thank him for me, Naomi." Edward admired Angus' handiwork.

"I already have. I told him that he could have the day off after he finished stocking the woodpile."

"You are becoming quite the mistress of Brachney Hall."

Naomi sat down beside him. "It does not hurt to practice. Allison and the Zigmanns would have joined us on Sunday, but they are hosting a taffy pull at the cottage for the Wheaton children. Remind me to give that bag of Allison's clothes to her for the Wheaton girls. There are so many now, five, with another on the way. Perhaps they will have a son this time around...Edward, when I was in London at the dry goods store, there was this little, tattered lad viewing the stationery." Naomi got up and walked over to the table. "Of course the storekeeper was outraged and threw him out into the street. I cannot help wondering why the lad ventured in there in the first place. And why the paper section?" Edward stared into space. Naomi sat down again next to Edward.

Naomi continued, "Was he looking for a gift for his mother? Did he even have a mother? Maybe he just liked looking at all the beautiful designs; maybe he has artistic talent. Why there? Why not the candy section? Edward, what do you think? Edward?"

"Uh...I agree that the Wheaton's need not send out notes to announce the birth of their babies, just candy," Edward answered lamely.

"Edward Caleb McDonnally, you have not heard a word that I have said." Naomi left the chair beside him and replaced the cardholder to the mantle. "Do you like children, Edward?"

"Of course, everyone likes children."

Naomi turned to him and rolled her eyes.

"Naomi, are you asking me if I *like* children?"

"No, Edward that is why I inquired as to if you *liked* children?" she clarified sarcastically. "Edward sometimes you are absolutely intolerable." She turned to the window overlooking the front drive.

"Come here, love," he commanded gently.

Naomi meandered leisurely back to her place beside him.

"Yes, Naomi Beatrice McDonnally, I do love children, especially ours."

The mention of Naomi's shared name with her mother, Beatrice, who had disappeared mysteriously when Naomi was a child in Newcastle, sent Naomi to thoughts of a wedding day without the loving woman.

"Naomi?"

"Yes, Edward?"

"Now who's preoccupied? Where were you?"

"Thinking of our wedding."

"My stupidity may have delayed it, but you will have your wedding. Now, are you interested in my answer, or not, Mrs. McDonnally?"

"What answer, Edward?"

"To your question about children?"

"Oh that...I am not sure that I am prepared for your answer."

"Naomi, what would you like me to say?"

"Something of your honest feelings. I am over thirty and you are a bit older. And we do have Allison and she is a grown woman."

"Are you saying that you are not interested in enlarging our family, Naomi?"

"No, I just wanted your thoughts on the subject."

"Are you certain?"

"Yes, Edward."

"Well then, my magic square, the fact is that I am eight years your senior, but I do not consider myself to be an old man yet. I have a few good years left in me— well maybe not this year," he indicated as he gazed down at his broken limbs. But my honest feeling is—"

"Yes, Edward?"

"If you do not want more children, that is fine with me."

"It is?" Naomi asked solemnly.

"Or if you care to adopt a few, that is also fine with me."

"I see," she dropped her head.

"But, if you want to have a child with me, after we are remarried, naturally, that would be perfect, too."

"Oh Edward...yes, yes, yes!" She threw her arms around him and smothered him in kisses.

"Yes, which is it?"

"I would love to have your child! Naomi squealed. "As soon as we are married, again.".

As they hugged and sealed the plan with an extended kiss, the sound of a clearing throat interrupted from the hall. The couple turned quickly to see their daughter standing before them.

"I did not mean to intrude," Allison apologized with an unquestionable smile.

"Then you approve, Baby?"

She ran to join them and hug them. "I would love to have a little sister or brother! After you are remarried," she laughed.

A few hours later, Hiram drove Daniel to the small northern village of Cranstoncliff. There Daniel purchased a series of antique books from an elderly priest. Hiram bought a Tolstoy first edition for Abigail, but insisted that *Daniel* deliver it to her when they returned the next day. Their visit to the village was pleasant, the weather unexpectedly favorable and the rural food excellent.

They returned early Sunday, after which Daniel spent a fair part of the afternoon visiting with his sister while Hiram attended to business matters.

After dinner, Hiram inquired about Abigail's health and invited Daniel to a game of darts, before their engagement at Brachney Hall. Random small talk kept any additional conversation of Daniel's sister at bay. Hiram opened the wooden box and removed the darts, giving Daniel his allotment.

"April twenty-third is William Shakespeare's birthday, Hiram." Daniel chose a dart and took aim with a successful throw.

"Very good shot...I was not aware of that, Daniel." Hiram followed suit, however his throw was pathetically poor.

"Sorry ol' man...Indeed, I have been plannin' a promotional sale o' his classics at the store, servin' cake and drink." Daniel took his turn with his dart landing very close to the center.

"Excellent shot and an excellent idea, Daniel." Hiram chose another dart, trying to concentrate for better accuracy. His efforts were once again in vain. Disturbed with the result he changed the subject. "How was your visit at Edward's yesterday?"

"Very entertainin'. I met Guillaume. Good lad." Daniel aimed carefully making another successful score.

"Yes, immature at times, not unlike the rest of us. He has potential as an excellent architect." Hiram said turning the dart over in his hand, with notable distraction.

"He hopes to visit the shoe factory that a man name o' Gropius designed wi' steel reinforced concrete. So light it can float."

"I should commission Guillaume to use it in redesigning the MacBride Bridge; it is forever in ill repair." *This one is for you Abigail.* Hiram drew his hand back and with a powerful thrust, the dart sped to the board and pierced the target dead on center.

"Aye. Bull's-eye! Congratulations, ol' friend, me thought ya were losin' ya touch. What inspired ya?"

"I do not like to lose," he said staring into space then returned. "We should prepare to leave for my uncle's. I am certain that our punctuality would be appreciated." Hiram took the darts and placed them in the wooden box.

"Abby—" Daniel stopped with Hiram's instant look of disapproval and decided that it was not the proper time to mention the delivery of the book, which Hiram gave to her.

"I will be in my room, Daniel. We should leave well before six."

Chapter XVI

"War and Peace"

"Nothing is more true, more real,
than the primeval magnetic disturbances
that two souls may communicate
to one another, through the tiny sparks
of a moment's glance."

—Victor Hugo

Sunday evening, Hiram arrived punctually at Abigail's room to escort her to the carriage. A myriad of conflicting thoughts filled his head. *Sophia says Abigail cares for me, yet she tries my temper at every turn. Has she once treated me with ill manners, since I found her on the ridge? No, she has been very agreeable. I adore her...but is hers only a physical attraction? She really does not know me.* Hiram paused at the door, feeling in a state of limbo, and then knocked. Eloise opened the door. He stepped in, his heart skipping a beat at the sight before him. There Abigail sat on the edge of the bed, well rested and looking refreshed and lovelier than ever. She was dressed beautifully in the color green, which highlighted the fire in her thick red hair, falling down over her shoulders. Hiram hesitated at the threshold, spellbound.

Eloise interrupted his fixation, "Her brother has gone to find Miss Sophia. Sir, are you not going to fetch Miss O'Leardon?"

"Aye...you are looking well, Miss O'Leardon. Are you ready?" *A foolish question... Look at you...my torment will continue throughout the evening.* Hiram approached the bed withholding any expression.

"Yes...thank you." *Only well? Do you not find me appealing? Have I blinded you with my...with my honesty?*

Hiram offered Abigail his arm, when the enchanting scent of her perfume filled his head, cutting away at his defenses. Abigail took his arm, walked comfortably with him to the hall, and closed her eyes with the disturbing thoughts.

This all feels too natural, too perfect... yet, I want to speak to you while we are alone. What shall I say? Time is running out. Perhaps I should thank you for the book?

Hiram's heart was racing with the very touch of her arm on his. His pace gradually decreased until he reached the last step. He could avoid her no longer. He slowly turned his head to meet her eyes, which melted into his, now dark and stern.

What do you expect from me, Abigail? Do you have the strength to overcome your fears? I am not certain that I can overcome mine.

Time stood still.

Hiram McDonnally, why do you look at me with such severity? Please, tell me what you are thinking. Do you find me at all acceptable?

Then the Master of McDonnally Manor made a decision without regard for their engagement at Brachney Hall. He led Abigail forward to the study that loomed ahead. They stopped in front of the doors and he reached to slide them open with his free hand. The grandfather clock chimed. Hiram stopped, listening to the ominous timepiece. Demanding its presence to be known and the memories to return, it continued to mark the hour, unrelenting, as it did so many years ago. Hiram's thoughts flashed back to his youth: first to those lost hours with Naomi, then to the heartbroken Allison and finally to Elizabeth with the closing door of flat number eight.

Abigail wondered, studying Hiram's face as he revisited his displeasing past, *what memories haunt you? What is happening? What were you planning?*

Hiram returned to present day and looked down to Abigail's concerned expression.

No, no Abigail, I am not prepared for this. Not at all. I shan't tell you how I feel. Not until I know what you truly think of me. I will not fall into that trap again. Embarrassed that he nearly conceded to what he deemed to be "irrational behavior", he redirected his pace to the main door and opened it.

Hiram walked Abigail out toward the carriage. The powerful winds caught her scarf, blowing it from her head. Hiram saw it flapping wildly, stopped in the portal, and rearranged the scarf over her head, his eyes never meeting hers as he slid the silk around her neck. He offered her his arm and they continued to the carriage. Once inside, Abigail slid across the seat to make room for her escort. However, Hiram took the seat across from her, keeping her at arm's length, but in perfect view. Daniel arrived shortly and climbed into the carriage, in the seat next to his sister.

Hiram gave a slight nod, unable to break his gaze from the vision of beauty across from him and then asked her brother, "Daniel, have you seen Sophia?"

"I passed her on the stairs. She went to fetch a heavier wrap. Abby, yer lookin' like the first breath o' spring. Do ye not agree Hiram?"

Hiram did not remark, surprised at Daniel's similar analogy with the season.

Abigail modestly dropped her head. *Well, speak. Do you agree with him?*

"Aye, words cannot express what my eyes perceive," Hiram replied mysteriously.

Was that a compliment? Abigail questioned and then looked up to see Sophia opening the carriage door.

Sophia viewed the seating arrangements with a troubled frown. "Oh, no, this will never do. Abigail, you will have to exchange seats. I cannot ride backwards, I get intolerably ill."

"Sophia, it is for a period of less than five

minutes." Hiram glared at his niece, fearing that even a few minutes sitting next to the lovely Miss O'Leardon could prove to be dangerous.

"Uncle Hiram, I am sure that you do not want to be responsible for ruining my evening. Now, I would ask to exchange seats with Daniel, but anyone can see that it would be nearly impossible for two handsome men, such as you, of such *large stature*, to comfortably occupy this very small seat. Uncle, could you please offer Abigail some assistance to the seat next to you, so that I could escape the cold and join you."

Hiram hesitated, and then offered Abigail a hand in moving to the seat on his left.

"Please hurry, it is awfully cold out here, Uncle Hiram." Daniel slid over and casually covered his mouth to hide his grin while he offered Sophia a hand.

Hiram was now provoked nearly one-step too far. He helped his conspiring niece to her seat, feeling that he was pandering to her every whim. He was tempted to leave the carriage and resort to walking, but managed to overcome his frustration and sat next to Abigail. Her scent, once again, challenged his defensive blockade. Finding his baulking, personally offensive, Abigail scooted toward the window allotting the maximum space between her and the apparently "disapproving" passenger.

"Is this not perfect?" Sophia remarked cheerfully.

Daniel observed that "perfect" it was not and dreaded that the predicted friction between his sister and friend was returning to its natural state. The concerned brother shook his head and took a moment for a quick silent prayer. Hiram tapped the carriage top and Albert drove the foursome to Brachney Hall.

At Edward's estate, Daniel was helping Sophia down from the carriage when a brushing wind swept past her head, followed by a crow's threatening screech. Sophia ran for the door under Daniel's protection.

"Ghastly beast!" Daniel swung at the terrorizing bird. "Better get inside, Sophia." Daniel opened the door without knocking and announced as they entered in haste. "Edward, ya have a mad bird in yer drive. It nearly attacked Sophia!" Hiram quickly rushed Abigail inside.

"Hello, Miss O'Leardon. Not a very hospitable welcome, I am afraid. I am Edward McDonnally, at your not so accommodating service. Pardon me for not rising," Edward smiled and bowed his head.

"My pleasure. I am Abigail," she smiled in return.

"Hiram, I see that you were not to be outdone by the likes of your handsome uncle. Naomi did not mention it." Edward said jovially.

Hiram's face reddened, confused by the implication until Edward explained, "The beard, Hiram. Or shall I say the lack of it. Pity the women of all Britain now. Any resistance they had for you before will be lost for sure!" Edward glanced to Abigail. Hiram modestly half-smiled, again displaying the previously veiled, dimples. Edward's speculation was accurate as Hiram's appealing change in appearance continued to weaken and threaten Abigail's fortress.

"What is this about a mad bird, Daniel?" Edward asked.

"A crow, black as pitch, lookin' as evil as the devil himself." Daniel replied.

Mention of the crow threw Edward back to the unpleasant event with the ladder. *The same blasted bird?* Eying the attractive Miss O'Leardon, he shook off the annoying memory and signaled Hiram to come closer. Naomi took Abigail's wrap. Hiram joined his uncle when Edward motioned for his nephew to lean down to hear his whispers.

"Hiram, why in the world would you want a cure for snakebites from that beauty? I should think a snake charmer would be more in order."

Hiram grinned slightly, thinking, *if you only knew, Edward.* Hiram excused himself and helped Naomi with the tray of refreshments after she invited everyone to the table to begin their pinochle game. "Hiram, please slide Abigail's chair closer to the table."

"Naomi, I am sorry, I do not play. I will watch," Abigail said regretfully.

Sophia jumped in immediately, evaluating the circumstances. "Well, I do and I choose Daniel for my partner! Uncle you will have to sit this one out."

"Sorry old man," Edward announced, trying to withhold a telltale grin.

Hiram looked nervously around the room, and then took the only available chair next to Abigail. Naomi opened the box of cards and began shuffling them when there was a knock at the door.

"Probably, that bird, tryin' to fool us," Daniel joked. Sophia looked fearfully down at the ring. Naomi stood, but Hiram obliged and greeted the new arrivals.

"Miss O'Connor... Mr. Zigmann." Hiram's narrowed eyes met Guillaume's as he recalled the young man's role in Elizabeth Clayton's retreat. Allison stood flabbergasted in the doorway, staring blankly at her clean-shaven companion of the past.

Guillaume noted Allison's response and stepped possessively closer to her. His nudge awoke her from the dazed confusion.

"Come in," Hiram graciously offered.

The guests entered. "Good evening. I had a— we had a few minutes before the Wheatons were to arrive. We thought that we would drop by and say hello." Allison stole one more glance at Hiram.

All exchanged greetings and then Edward asked, "Guillaume how is your head and the ribs?"

"I feel fine except, I think that Rusty and I may have exchanged places. *I* am the one that is taken for walks now, but I am trusted to go without the leash," Guillaume teased. Allison gave him a little scowl and a playful push.

"If you need anything else, remember I am taking care of your medical bills," Edward offered.

"I was thinking about a larger basket by the stove, I am a little cramped in Rusty's," Guillaume prodded.

"You are so very amusing, Mr. Zigmann." Allison muttered. The rest of the group found his comments quite entertaining. "Speaking of dogs, Mother, we have taken Heidi to the cottage to play with Rusty and the Wheaton children."

"That is fine. Any sign of a nasty crow out there? It attempted to attack Sophia," Naomi added, placing the cardholder in front of Edward.

"No. Were you hurt Sophie?" Guillaume inquired.

"No, thank you for asking. It will take a great deal more than some bizarre bird to ruffle my feathers," Sophia said half-heartedly.

"What kind of contraption is that, Edward?" Guillaume inquired inspecting the cardholder.

"Just a little tool, Angus rigged for me," Edward said proudly.

"Clever, yes," Allison cut in, "but we do not want to interrupt. Do we Guillaume? Go on with your game." Guillaume and Allison stepped to the side of the table to watch Naomi deal the cards.

As each player studied his or her hand, Sophia raised her hand closer to her face. With this gesture, Edward's eyes widened and his flabbergasted outburst startled everyone in the room. Once again, all eyes went to Sophia's hand.
"Sophia, where did you get that ring!"

Naomi looked over at Allison who was equally shocked in seeing Sophia donning what the villages believed to be Edward's token of appreciation for his mending lady, Harriet Dugan.

"*Guillaume* gave it to me," she looked to the unsuspecting young man, pleading for his corroboration. Questioning faces led Sophia to encourage him further, "Is that not so, Guillaume?"

"No, I certainly did not!"

"You most certainly did! *Remember*, as a friend?" she demanded his support.

Edward stared at the jewel in disbelief. Hiram and Abigail were at a loss to the significance of Sophia's possession, but the tides of doubt were rising between Edward and Guillaume and more so, between Guillaume and Allison. Once again, their recent reunion as a trusting couple was being tested for its strength.

"Guillaume, did you, or did you not give the ring to Sophia?" Allison commanded sharply.

"I did not!"

"I believe you, Guillaume. Sophia, we *will* discuss this later. We need to be going." Allison added with unfettered ease.

Relieved, Guillaume grinned proudly and shook his head in perplexed disappointment with Sophia. He shrugged his shoulders when Edward bid him a reluctant farewell, Guillaume being Edward's only confidant with the knowledge of the ring, originally intended for Naomi. Edward needed answers but knew that this was not the appropriate time or place. He was ready to put the matter to rest when he saw the vengeful crow sitting on the windowsill. The sight of the mischievous creature, cast a new light on the dilemma. It was all beginning to make sense— the missing ring and the vicious attack on his niece. He understood the situation, but did not have a clue as to how to handle it. *Later,* he thought.

Hiram and Abigail sat unassuming and ignoring one another. Finally, Abigail brought up one of Hiram's most dreaded subjects. "I met with Allison, yesterday."

"Yes, I am aware of that, I—"

"All right, this is not acceptable," Sophia cut her uncle off.

"Sophia!" Hiram reprimanded.

"I apologize Uncle, but I am in need of full concentration, in order to play this hand properly. I owe that to my partner, your dearest friend. If you please, could you escort Abigail to another room to converse? We would all be in your debt," she added diplomatically.

Before Hiram had an opportunity to object, the others chimed in.

"Yes, that would be a good idea, the pain in my arm is distracting enough," Edward grinned placing his cards in the slots of the new cardholder.

"It has been a time since I have played, Hiram. A wee bit o' silence would be appreciated,"

Daniel agreed, flipping through his cards.

After a slight nudge from Edward's good foot, Naomi suggested, "Hiram, you may take Abigail into the library. You will not disturb anyone there." Hiram's expression became sour and displeased with the ambush.

Likewise, Abigail, was at a loss with the solidarity of the card players, but agreed to leave with Hiram. "That will be fine," she said with very little enthusiasm.

Hiram lost all poise and stubbornly offered his arm. Ignoring her enticing fragrance, he accompanied her to the library as though she were a disturbed beehive with its swarm ready to attack. There they found one small couch. Interestingly enough, all the other chairs were mysteriously missing. Both suspected foul play.

"Hmm," Hiram questioned when Abigail took a place on the couch. Intimidated by the solitude with Abigail, Hiram immediately began circling the room, looking over the extensive book collection.

"Allison is a fine young woman," Abigail remarked, waiting for Hiram's reaction.

Hiram mumbled and chose a novel from the shelf at the end of the room, "Yes, she is. Very independent, very much like yourself."

"I beg your pardon, I did not hear."

He raised the volume of his voice, "I said that Allison is very independent, not unlike you!"

A voice from the drawing room called out, "A little quieter in there, please." Hiram slammed the book shut and put it back on the shelf, with the request.

"It may be easier to converse, if you sit," Abigail pointed out. Considering the seating arrangements, Hiram ignored the invitation, moved nearer and continued poring over the shelves.

Abigail took offense, "Suit yourself." She sat with her hands folded in her lap. "Your uncle *is* very charming. Would you get me that footstool, please?" she requested, nearly shouting.

Only in the name of chivalry, Hiram rationalized taking a deep breath. He placed the footstool in front of her. She raised her feet. He unconsciously lingered, tempted by her disturbing radiance.

"Thank you. This couch can accommodate both of us...You once gave me a lecture on civility, might we practice it now?"

Abigail's hint to his hypocrisy, forced Hiram to respond as a proper gentleman. He looked over the available space and sat down next to her.

"Daniel gave me the Tolstoy novel. Thank you, Mr. McDonnally."

"It was the very least that I could do, considering..."

"I thought it to be an interesting title...
that you chose...to give to me," Abigail said suspiciously.

"Is there nothing that satisfies you!" Hiram left the couch. He jerked the volume, *Oscar Wilde's the Happy Prince and other Stories.* from the shelf and announced, "Maybe this would have been more to your liking!" and held it up for her to read. Abigail sat open-mouthed.

She scoffed, "I think that *Dr. Jekyll and Mr. Hyde* would be a more fitting gift from you."

"Very clever, very clever, indeed, Miss O'Leardon." He returned to her side. "So, I am the one with the dual personality, one minute you are brow beating me, the next you are comparing me to—"

"Mr. McDonnally, I am astounded. How do you come up with these ridiculous accusations? Do not trouble yourself with an answer. I was not the one that invited someone to share the afternoon at Duncan Ridge, and then invited a score of eligible dance partners to humiliate that very same person on that very same day!" Abigail folded her arms in disgust. "Do not deny it! Your niece told me of your despicable scheme!"

The shock of her statement demanded a reply. Hiram walked over to the couch and stared down at her. "Humiliate?" he shouted.

Another voice echoed from the drawing room, "We are trying to play a serious game of cards in here!"

"Yes, *humiliate!* Maybe I should have requested that Naomi invite Ian MacGill!" Abigail added fuel to the fire. Hiram folded his arms and stood confidently.

"In the first place, neither Naomi, nor my uncle would ever allow that criminal savage, into their house! Secondly, I cannot imagine why you would consider inviting someone who you believe to be one thousand times less handsome than myself and yet expect me to become jealous with his presence?"

"I never said a thousand, I said *ten!*" Abigail inadvertently admitted, falling into his trap. Hiram refrained from displaying a smile of victory. "Mr. McDonnally, I am not amused." His sparkling eyes quickly destroyed her first line of defense. She looked away, "You grate on my nerves."

Hiram sat down next to her. "I am certain that I affect your nervous system and I admit that my tactics are not always conventional."

"Tactics? Strategy for the battlefield? Is this a war game we are playing, Mr. McDonnally?

"No…Miss O'Leardon. It is not a game, not of any nature. I discovered *that*, when I found you frightened, shivering in the cold, because of my negligence."

Abigail sat stunned, with the twist in the conversation. She felt his dark eyes creeping into her soul seeking confirmation of his failure. Her conscience retaliated restoring her flippant attitude to one of respect.

"I take full responsibility for my suffering, Mr. McDonnally. I chose to stay behind."

"Miss O'Leardon, I treated you with unconscionable disrespect and tyranny at Duncan Ridge. My actions were equivalent to those of primitive man, dragging you off against your will."

"It is quite a task dragging off a stubborn mule," Abigail said lightly.

"That paints an interesting picture. Is that what this relationship has become? A crazed caveman dragging a mule around all of Scotland?" Hiram's endearing smile slowly surfaced, capturing her heart.

Abigail dropped her head to escape his attentive gaze.

Hiram leaned back and folded his hands in his lap.

"Sophia, told you, did she not?" Abigail inquired humbly.

"About?"

"My comments, in the village."

"A detailed account," he said casually.

"I shan't deny it."

"And I shan't deny that my motive for inviting the ladies was purely one of revenge, to make you jealous."

"Jealous?"

"Ardently."

Abigail refused to face him. " I should explain that my experiences with relationships have not been pleasant, Mr. McDonnally."

"I choose to describe mine as tragedies." Hiram turned to her. "Abby, I never meant to hurt you... Granted, I have made more than my share of mistakes, undoubtedly, in every relationship, including ours. However, after these last few weeks, despite our disputes and our quarrels, I found that the more you taunted me the more I was determined to win your approval. To ignore you was inconceivable."

"A challenge? Is that all I am to you?" Two tiny wrinkles appeared between Abigail's brows with defiance.

"I shan't deny that my ego was in need of repair, but do you not think that it would have been more beneficial for me to pursue a woman requiring a little less tolerance? Less verbal, perhaps?" his eyes twinkled.

"Perhaps not. I have met but three of the women of your past and it is all very apparent to me."

"Inform me, Miss O'Leardon." Hiram leaned back, resigned to listen to her explanation.

"Very well. Naomi is a wonderful woman and very sweet. My perception is that she was too tolerant. I would suspect that she never raised her voice on the day that you destroyed the parlor and I would further venture to guess that Naomi never fought you for the relationship. She let you walk away. Am I correct?"

"Yes. Continue, if you dare, despite my untamed temper," he grinned.

"Miss Elizabeth Clayton, on the other hand, was interesting enough, I am sure. However, unlike Naomi she spoke, but with vague obscurity. She probably never invited you into her flat that last evening in London. She left you standing in the hall with your flowers or a box of candy, did she not?"

Hiram remained silent, without rebuttal. He leaned forward resting his elbows on his knees and head in his hand. Abigail waited for him to respond, fearing that she may have hit a nerve. Each passing minute held the potential of the calm before a storm.

"Yes," he said without expression.

"Now," she began slowly with greater apprehension. "I believe that Allison's ability to articulate really had no bearing in your relationship. That was an entirely different situation. Having met Naomi and Elizabeth, I do not believe that you ever had any romantic ties with Allison. She was too young. The perfect relationship, for you, *then*. It was safe, requiring no true commitment Is this true?" Hiram leaned back.

"Tact is your forte, Miss O'Leardon. Quite useful in dissection of the male character."

"If I am anything, I am verbal. Honesty is essential in every relationship. Do you not agree?"

"Aye...honesty, the double edged sword. It can be the foundation and fortitude of a relationship and yet it has the power to obliterate it in a second's time... Very well, you have chosen your weapon. Might I reciprocate? I spent most of my life alone. I tend to miscalculate and misunderstand women." Hiram got up and walked a few steps, then turned to Abigail.

"At this very moment, Miss O'Leardon, my greatest fear is to bare my soul to you."

Abigail looked on mercifully, admiring his sincerity. *You really do not know, do you?* Abigail slowly shook her head. "Please sit down, Hiram."

He suspected a negative tone in her words unbearably similar to that of Naomi's on that dreaded day in the parlor and to that of Elizabeth's on that last night in London— that gentleness, yet sound of doom in her voice. His feet would not move, his heart was heavy in his chest, his eyes fixed on hers, pleading in silence that she not bring an end to his dream, even if it meant continuing the battles in this ongoing war. *I will not sit; I will not make this easy for you. I will fight for this!*

"No, Abigail, I will not sit, nor will I stand for this!"

"One moment," Abigail begged and stood before him.

"You are not going anywhere, Abigail O'Leardon." He looked down to her, unrelenting. "You may be as stubborn as a mule, but you are dealing with a McDonnally. If perfection is what you seek, yes, you will need to seek it elsewhere." He searched her face for signs of approval. He reached out, his hands trembling, and took hers in his. "I may appear to be a man flawed with failings," his voice cracked, "but I assure you that the Almighty has provided me with one blessing that no other man on this earth can claim...I have the ability to see beyond your unmatched beauty and blatant cynicism— to see deep into your soul, which mirrors my own." His hands tightened around hers. "Aye, our pasts threaten our daily behavior— our every action and every word which passes through our lips. You and I, Abigail, have constructed impenetrable walls surrounding our egos to protect ourselves from even the smallest of cupid's arrows."

Her eyes, intense with interest, dropped from his. *Extraordinary man,* she thought, surrendering to his eloquent words. Her fingers slid from his as she sat down to the couch with defeat. "I believe that I may have been grossly unfair in judging you, sir."

"My mother taught me to withhold judgment...if at all possible."

Abigail turned her face away in shame, with his pointed comment refusing to make any eye contact with him. Hiram quickly realized that his last comment had been misconstrued as criticism. He knelt down on the floor before her, lamenting the offense. Abigail tried to hide her despair, initiated by his perceived disappointment in her lack of virtue, but failed as her eyes welled up.

Meanwhile, Sophia could not resist the temptation to investigate the silence in the library. She excused herself to the kitchen and entered the hall, then tiptoed to the doorway of the library and peeked in. Her hand flew to her mouth in shock then she fled back to the card table beaming ecstatically.

"What is it Sophia?" Naomi asked.

"We succeeded, Uncle Hiram is proposing to her!"

"You heard him?" Edward leaned forward.

"I saw him, down on the floor at her feet!"

"This is me dream come true. Abby findin' the perfect husband, none other than me dearest friend," Daniel smiled ear to ear.

Edward put his arm around Naomi and smiled confidently. At long last, his uncertainties with his nephew's past feelings for Naomi would be dissolved. He exchanged satisfied smiles with Sophia. Then the story behind the jewel flashing on his niece's hand returned to haunt him.

"May I call you *Uncle,* too?" Sophia asked Daniel.

"I would like nothin' more!"

The card game went on with less enthusiasm as every player anxiously awaited the return of the blessed couple.

.   Hiram reached over to lay his hand on Abigail's. She moved away from his touch and his prying eyes.

"Miss O'Leardon? I meant nothing derogatory. Remember me?" he whispered. "The caveman that is a thousand times more handsome than MacGill."

"I said only ten," she mumbled.

"Only, ten, Miss O'Leardon? You cut me to the quick," he said pitifully.

"Perhaps, ten *thousand*, Mr. McDonnally," her tiny grin gradually emerged in forgiveness.

Hiram stood, took her hands, lifted her from her position, and brought them slowly to his lips and kissed one, then the other. Abigail cocked her head in disbelief.

"Abigail, honesty is indeed a virtue. May I be so bold to believe that you would choose to have this war come to an end?"

Abigail listened intently to his plea. *Hiram, you are more than I ever imagined. It is true, you are not like the others.* Her focus fell to the cherished sight of her hands lovingly enclosed in those of her battling opponent.

With a worrisome expression, Hiram continued, "Do we not share the same hopes and dreams— to love and be loved?"

Abigail's fears were eased as an omnipotent trust slowly tore down the wall between them. The young lad within Hiram begged him to break free and flee, but the man inside, who had spent most of his life alone, demanded he stay and fight until the bitter end. Hiram slowly brought her hands to rest in his, next to his chest.

"Do you feel the pain in my heart? Can we not leave our pasts behind? I have never desired your honesty, more than I do at this very moment. Tell me the truth, Abby. May the future be ours?"

Although, Abigail knew that she had the power to destroy him with a word, instead, she prayed for the perfect reply. She smiled serenely when her thoughts returned to their first day at the café.

"If you so desire, Master McDonnally," she affirmed sweetly.

Hiram moved closer, driven by the love that he had harbored for what seemed to be eternity. He gently lifted her hands to his shoulders and drew her slowly to his chest. The pounding of their hearts intensified as his lips brushed across her cheek, down toward hers. All anger, fear and frustration faded as his hands guided her face to his for that tender kiss, which had always been only a breath away. They closed their eyes sealing the pact for peace and hope.

Hiram and Abigail embraced, bonded in a silent truce with their thoughts, like the pleasant tinkling of glass chimes in a spring breeze.

Miss O'Leardon, victory is mine. You *now belong to me.*

Mr. McDonnally, the war is over. I *have won.*

Sophia stood in the doorway beaming with delight.

"See the mountains kiss high heaven,
   And the waves clasp one another;
No sister flower would be forgiven
   If it disdained its brother;
And the sunlight clasps the earth
And the moonbeams kiss the sea;
What are all these kissings worth,
   If thou kiss not me?"

—Percy Bysshe Shelley

"The sound of a kiss is not so loud
as that of a cannon, but its echo
lasts a great deal longer."

—Oliver Wendell Holmes

Non-fictional facts referenced in Spring Spirit

Percheron and Hannoverian Horses
Duncan Phyfe chair
"Flicka" common Swedish name for dogs, meaning "little girl"
Melbourne, Australia
Peter Pan Statue in Kensington Gardens
Popularity of foxtrot
Buckingham Palace
The Thames
Tower of London
Westminster Abbey
Birmingham
Castle at Nottingham
Manchester
Midlands: black-faced sheep, stone cottages
Damp tea leaves to absorb carpet dust
Milk delivery details
Dan Patch and details
The Wasp and *The International 500 Mile Sweepstakes Race* and details
Tilting pitcher
Heated stone pig
Zane Grey's novel *Riders of the Purple Sage*
Alcohol burning coffee percolator
Popularity of pinochle card games, darts and taffy pulls
Invention of the recliner, *The Royal Chair*
Architect –Gropias and design details
April 23- William Shakespeare's birthday
L. Tolstoy's novel *War and Peace*
Sherlock Holmes mysteries
Dr. Jekyll and Mr. Hyde

Poetry Excerpts from the Chapters

Acknowledgements

Chronicle of the 20th Century.
New York: Chronicle Publications, 1987

Grun, Bernard. The Timetables of History: A
Horizontal Linkage of People and Events.
New York: Simon and Schuster, 1982.

Illustrated Encyclopedia of Scotland.
Anacortes,: Oyster Press, 2004.

Kidd, Dorothy. To See Ourselves. Edinburgh:
HarperCollins, 1992

Lacayo, Richard & Russell, George. Eyewitness
150 Years of Journalism. New York: Time Inc.
Magazine Company, 1995.

Summers, Gilbert. Exploring Rural Scotland.
Lincolnwood: Passport Books, 1996

Webster's International Encyclopedia. Naples:
Trident Press International, 1996.

Webster's New Biographical Dictionary.
Springfield: Merriam-Webster Inc, 1988.

A NOTE FROM THE AUTHOR:

I am a firm believer
that education should be an ongoing endeavor.
I stand by the unwritten law
that education should be entertaining
for young and old alike.
Thus, I incorporate
historic places, people and events
in my novels
for your learning pleasure.

With loving thoughts,
Arianna Snow

To order
Patience, My Dear
My Magic Square
and
Spring Spirit

Visit the Golden Horse Ltd.
website :
www.ariannaghnovels.com

Watch for the fourth
in the series!

**Note to the reader: You may be wondering why this book, with the same size font and with only eight more pages than the previous volume, took much longer for you to read.

The answer: the layout and over 5,000 more words.